ALSO BY LEIA STONE

FALLEN ACADEMY

YEAR TWO

LEIA STONE

Bl**oo**m *books*

Published by Bloom Books, an imprint of Sourcebooks
P.O. Box 4410, Naperville, Illinois 60567-4410
(630) 961-3900
sourcebooks.com

Originally self-published in 2018 by Leia Stone LLC.

Cataloging-in-Publication data is on file with the Library of Congress.

The authorized representative in the EEA is Dorling Kindersley
Verlag GmbH. Arnulfstr. 124, 80636 Munich, Germany

Manufactured in the UK by Clays and distributed by
Dorling Kindersley Limited, London
001-350256-Apr/25
10 9 8 7 6 5 4 3 2 1

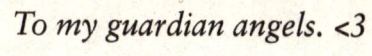

To my guardian angels. <3

CHAPTER 1

"Hustle, Atwater!" Lincoln screamed in my ear as I ran along a track behind the school.

I shot him a death glare and took off, making it to the front of the line where Tiffany was running like a freaking gazelle, not a drop of sweat to be seen. I side-glanced at my fellow blonde nemesis. One foot stuck out and she would trip—and at this speed, she'd probably break her nose. Maybe even a tooth.

"Stop and drop!" Lincoln shouted.

I growled and skidded to a halt. All plans of rearranging Tiffany's face were ruined, as our group of twenty boot camp cadets dropped to the ground, and started to do push-ups. The gravel ate into the palms of my hands, but I knew better than to complain.

Shea had dropped a few feet behind me. "Your boyfriend is a psycho," she whispered.

I didn't have the extra breath to reply.

We'd been at boot camp for a month. The eighty-eight students who passed the gauntlet had been separated into four groups, with either Lincoln, Noah, Blake, or Darren as their drill sergeant.

Guess which group I got?

"Faster!" Lincoln barked.

Boot camp was supposed to prepare us for joining the Fallen Army. The paychecks had started to come in, and I wasn't going to lie, it was nice. We were kind of like reserve army members. We would still finish school here at Fallen Academy, but one weekend a month we'd go out into the war zone and help flush out the demons that were ravaging the humans there. And of course, in an emergency, we'd be called out too.

I was just settling into the summer nicely. It took a few weeks for the stares at the devil mark on my chest to die down. Tiffany now called me Princess of Darkness as well as Archie. Her payback was coming—Shea was brewing a gnarly potion that would hopefully make her intestines fall out.

"*Up!*" Lincoln roared, and I sank to the ground, letting my burning arms take a moment of rest.

Lincoln's boots stopped two inches from my face. "Brielle Atwater, you are dismissed for the rest of the day." His voice was layered with concern.

What the...?

Jumping up, I got ready to defend myself regarding whatever I was in trouble for, when I looked just beyond him and saw my mom. She was standing there with my little brother, Mikey, who was hunched over. It looked like his face was bleeding.

Oh shit.

"Preferential treatment," Tiffany mumbled next to me, causing Lincoln to shoot a sharp glare at her.

"Give me two laps for speaking out of turn, Woods," he growled.

With a huff, she took off.

I looked up at my man with a thankful expression. "Thank you, sir!" I shouted, then started running to meet my family.

My mind was going through a thousand thoughts. *Did Grim—Shea's boss, who I'd almost killed and was now my mom's boss—attack Mikey? Did he just get jumped by demon thugs?*

As I neared, I saw two duffel bags behind them.

"What happened?" I skidded to a stop and took in the scene.

My mom looked fine. Tired, but normal. My brother, however, looked like he'd been beaten badly. His right eye was swollen, nose broken, lip split, and he was probably clutching broken ribs.

My mom chewed her lip. "He can't go back to Demon City. Some Tainted Academy kids roughed him up."

Those assholes! I would kill them.

"Mikey," I breathed, reaching out to touch his shoulder, but he recoiled.

"They said if I came back, they'd kill me," he grumbled.

My eyes widened. *What the hell? Are they somehow targeting him because he's my brother?*

My mom was staring at my chest and the mark that lay there in shock. I'd spoken to her on the phone several times after the gauntlet, told her what happened and explained the mark, but to see her staring at my chest now with tears in her eyes made my stomach hurt.

"Okay, we'll figure it out," I said to Mikey. The demons were clearly after my family.

Mikey swayed a little on his feet. He needed medical attention.

"Come on, let's get him to the clinic," I told my mom.

Mikey was eighteen now, which meant he'd be attending the Awakening ceremony in August. As a free soul, he'd be admitted to Fallen Academy. Maybe I could get him in a little earlier than planned.

While my mom helped Mikey limp to the healing clinic, I trailed after them with his duffel bags. After introducing Mrs. Greely to them, I paced while she scanned him for injuries. I hadn't yet learned the energetic scanning that could tell a healer if someone had internal wounds, such as bleeding or

4

tumors, as it was a third-year thing. I was eager to learn though.

Mrs. Greely winced. "Three broken ribs, but no internal bleeding. I'll need Noah to heal the nose and ribs, but I can get started on the rest."

Relief mixed with anger poured through me. How dare these bastards jump my little bro. Was it because they wanted to get to me? Was that their motive?

"I'll get Noah," I told her and bolted from the room, pulling my cell from my pocket.

He was out on the field screaming obscenities at his boot camp group no doubt, so I didn't expect him to pick up, but he did.

"Hey, Lincoln told me. I'm on my way," was all he said before he hung up.

What the...? Damn, my boyfriend was good. Sort of. When he wasn't torturing me.

I had barely even made it down the hall when the double doors opened, Noah striding through in all his beautiful perfection.

"What happened?" he asked.

I rubbed my sore arms, still burning from the push-ups. "Some kids at Tainted Academy jumped him."

Noah growled. "Little shits. Don't worry, I'll fix him up," he told me and then winked. This guy handed out winks like they were high fives.

I nodded. "Thank you."

5

He jogged down the hall and I just stayed there, letting my thoughts run rampant. My mom would have to go back, but Mikey needed to stay. There were still five weeks of summer before the Awakening ceremony. What was I going to do with him for five weeks?

I made $2700 a month with my new Fallen Army gig, but that wasn't enough for a studio apartment in Angel City. Especially after 50 percent taxes were taken out, plus my student health insurance, which was mandatory now that I was in the army. I needed some of that money for my own shit too—I was expected to have all these uniforms and military-grade boots, and that stuff wasn't cheap. The army surplus store gave student deals, but—

"Bri?" My mom's soft voice cut through my overthinking of the situation.

I spun, and upon seeing her open arms, I fell into them. Feeling her, smelling her, it made me emotional. I was homesick. I didn't get to see her enough, and having her here with me now was a welcome relief, even under these circumstances.

When I pulled back, she smiled down at me through tired eyes.

"I gotta get back. This was my lunch break," she said, her eyes flicking to the tattoo on my chest again. She didn't say a word though. When I'd told her over the phone, she'd cried, but my mom was the type of person who didn't dwell on bad shit. She just got over it and moved on. A useful survival tool.

"How's work?" I asked her. Since Lincoln killed her boss to dissolve my slave contract, she'd gotten a new boss—Mr. Grim, Shea's old boss who owned all the strip clubs.

"It's okay. Not making as much money as when Burdock was running it. Grim doesn't like that." She shrugged.

Panic gripped me. "Does he hurt you? Grim?"

She shook her head. "No. He leaves me be, but docks my pay for stupid things. He's all about the money."

That mofo!

Suddenly I felt selfish. Every time we spoke, we talked about me. Did my mom need money? "Well hey, I am a salaried Fallen Army soldier now, so I can help out with your bills," I told her.

Her limp blond hair fell across her shoulders, as she shook her head. "No, baby. I'll be okay. I rented out your and Shea's room about four months ago to Mrs. Conner. You just take care of Mikey, okay?"

Mikey. Shit. What am I going to do with him?

I nodded. "Of course, Mom. I will."

She smiled again, weaker that time. "Love you, bee." The childhood nickname caught me off guard. She hadn't called me bee or bumblebee since I was ten.

"Love you too, Mom." I pulled her in for another hug, but then all too soon she was drawing away.

"Bernie and Maximus miss you," she added, and

then she left. Just like that. She just left me with my little brother to take care of, and an ache in my heart for her, for Bernie, for all of them. It was the first time that I really realized how bad Demon City was, how bad being a slave bound was.

I smoothed my hair and left the healing unit in search of the only person I knew could, and would help Mikey.

I knocked on the large double doors lightly, praying he would be in his office.

"Come in!" Raphael's cheery voice called out.

Thank God.

Relief mixed with nerves flooded through me as I stepped into his office. He sat at his desk, looking over what looked to be maps and papers. He seemed surprised to see me.

"Brielle? Is everything all right?" he asked, standing up from the desk, and walking around to meet me. His huge white wings were always striking, and I found myself staring, transfixed, at them.

"Is someone hurt?" His concern deepened.

Damn, I forgot about the mind reading.

"Yeah, my brother. Who is a free soul!" I added quickly. "He was beat up by some Tainted Academy kids, and now...he can't go back to Demon City."

I let that linger for a minute. Raphael's brows

drew together with concern.

"*But* it's only five weeks until the Awakening, and since he's a free soul, he'll be coming to Fallen Academy anyway." *Unless he's a Gristle. Oh* God *please don't make him a Gristle.*

"So…" I couldn't do it. I couldn't ask.

Raphael chuckled. "You want him to stay here in the meantime?"

Relief poured through me once again. "Yes. Please. If that's okay?"

The archangel rubbed his chin and then consulted some of the papers on his desk. "We are still transitioning students who failed the gauntlet out of school. We've allowed them to stay for the summer in the dorm housing, but we are working to get them jobs and more permanent housing, so I don't have anything open at the moment."

My heart sank. I guess I could stay at Lincoln's and he could have my bed, but I doubted they would allow a guy in the girls' dormitory.

"Except." Raphael held up a hand. "Is he okay with doing yard work? Mowing the field, trimming hedges? My groundskeeper just graduated last year, and his cottage and job are open. Your brother could have the job for the summer, and give me time to find a replacement."

A fifty-pound weight lifted off my shoulders.

"Yes! Thank you, sir! He'll do anything you need. He's a super hard worker."

Not exactly the truth, but he could learn to become one. Maybe.

Raphael beamed. "Wonderful." Walking over to a cabinet, he produced a set of keys. "Here are the keys to the cottage. It's the one behind the gym."

So that's what it is. I'd seen it before and wondered what it was. It looked like a tiny stone house that had been left behind when they were building this enormous school.

"Thank you so much, sir."

My walk back to the healing clinic was a little bit lighter. I'd figured out a temporary situation for Mikey. Now, I just needed him to not be a Gristle.

When I got back to his room, he was knocked out, fast asleep. Noah was doing his crazy orange glowing hand, healing magic thing.

"He okay?" I asked as I heaved his two duffel bags over my shoulders.

Noah nodded. "Gave him a sedative. Mending bones is painful."

Yikes.

"Thanks a lot. I'll be right back, gonna set up his new living space," I told the healer.

I wasn't sure which was harder, Lincoln's drill team exercises or schlepping two huge, heavy duffel bags across campus to the little stone cottage.

By the time I got there, my arms were so fatigued they were shaking. I let myself in quickly, and then dumped the bags on the floor. One of the zippers split the second it landed, and I winced as all my brother's shit came tumbling out.

What a mess.

Leaning down to pick it up, my eyes fell on a bright orange flyer that had rolled out of his bag. The bold font stating $1,000,000 caught my eye first, then the words 'Fight Night.'

What the...?

I picked it up and scanned over the flyer.

FIGHT NIGHT

Winner gets $1,000,000

(no strings attached)

Teams of two fighters will face off.

Whoever is left standing wins.

Televised. Ages 18–21 only.

$100 entry fee per team.

Winners get invited to join the Tainted Army.

The last line made the room sway. Tainted Army? What the hell was that? I mean, it sounded a lot like Fallen Army, but...were the demons now using kids to fight for them beyond the wall? It was sickening.

My head was reeling, so I sat down for a second. As I leaned on the bed, I flipped the flyer over and my brother's messy handwriting made my heart jackknife in my chest.

Win the money. Buy mom's demon contract. Free soul.

I sat up straighter. Could my brother have been onto something? Would Mr. Grim take a million bucks to release my mom from her contract? She had just said he was all about the money...

I stood then, a fierce desire in my heart. I was going to win Fight Night and free my mom. But it was going to take some help.

Glancing at the paper, I noted the fight was scheduled for February, months away from today. I had time to plan.

Hang on, Mama. I'm coming for ya.

CHAPTER 2

"ABSOLUTELY NOT!" LINCOLN ROARED. THE sound was made louder by the fact that we were in his tiny trailer. It was late, and I just wanted this shit storm of a day to be over, but I couldn't lie to him. Besides, I would need his help.

"Babe." I had never used the pet name before, but maybe it would help soften the blow now. "I'm doing it regardless. I'm just asking you to help train me for the fight."

He looked furious. The veins in his neck were bulging, and his left eyelid was twitching. "You don't even know if he'll take the money!"

"He will," Shea, who had been quiet while we fought, spoke up at that point. "He's money motivated. I worked for him for nearly six years. If the Necro clinic isn't making much, then he'll see it as a fair payout for losing an employee. He'll hire a new Necro, and be happy with the deal."

Lincoln shot her a death glare. "Noah and I will fight," he finally answered.

I winced and pointed to the flyer. "It says eighteen to twenty-one. You guys are twenty-three." It was sweet of him to offer to fight for my mom though, which I would never forget.

His fingertips pressed against his temples, rubbing them. "Well, you're not doing it. We'll crowd fund or something."

I barked out a laugh. "Crowd fund a million bucks? People don't even like me! They think I'm evil. No one is going to pay to get my slave bound mom out of Demon City, Lincoln."

He sighed. "Well, it's a bad idea. You could die."

I chewed my lip and stepped closer to him, reaching out to touch his arm. "It's my *mom*, Lincoln. My flesh and blood. The woman who gave me life." *I saw* the moment he admitted defeat.

"You're going to be the death of me."

I grinned. "So you'll train me?"

Growling, he nodded. "Who's your fighting partner?"

Shea stood, popping her knuckles. "Ghetto Tainted Academy bitches got nothing on me," she stated matter-of-factly.

Lincoln sighed, looking at the ceiling as if it held

some answers. "We'll see about that. Meet me in the small gym every day after boot camp. Every. Day. Including weekends. And when school starts, I want you in there every day after school."

Shea groaned, and his eyes flicked to hers with a glare. "Just kidding. Yay." She fake-cheered.

Lincoln rubbed his temples. "Now go, before I change my mind."

We turned to leave, and his hand snaked out and pulled me into him. The moment his lips touched mine, I felt all my worries melt away. Lincoln had my back. If he trained us, we could totally, probably, win this.

When he pulled back, his cobalt eyes bored into mine. "I love you, Brielle. But please stop trying to die," he pleaded.

Giving him a thumbs-up, I smirked. "You got it. Just after this one thing."

With a roll of his eyes, he chuckled. "Good night." He kissed me one more time, making my knees go weak.

"Night." I grinned.

———•———

As Shea and I headed for Mikey's cottage to check on him, she gave me a side glance. "We can do this, right? Fight the Demon City kids? I mean, they are hardcore there…"

I knew she'd had it rough in the short time she'd spent at Tainted Academy, but I couldn't have her losing hope on me. Stopping to face her, I peered into her large brown eyes.

"We grew up in the same hood as they did. We know how to fight dirty, and we've gotten a much better education here. With Sera, and with your magic, I know we can win. For Mom."

Shea never called her by the name 'Mom,' always Kate, but she was like Shea's mother too.

"For Mom," she agreed with a smile.

Family was family. Blood didn't matter.

I gave her a hug, and then we walked briskly to the cottage where my brother was staying.

When we got to Mikey's, I knocked loudly, only just wondering if he might still be drugged up.

"Come in!" he shouted groggily.

Shea and I walked in to see him lying in bed, scrolling through his phone. He set it down and sat up slowly as we entered, still clutching his ribs.

"Thanks for getting me this place." He gestured to the room, but his face fell when his gaze landed on the piece of paper in my hands.

"Busted." I held up the flyer. Even though he was only a year younger than me, I still mothered him.

Looking up at me, he sighed. The bruising on his face was intense, but at least his nose looked normal again.

"Is this why the kids jumped you?" Shea asked, crossing her arms.

The thought hadn't even occurred to me.

He nodded. "I went to sign up. They said I was too much of a pussy and jumped me. Took my hundred bucks."

Well shit. Now I felt really bad for him, and also completely enraged that some Tainted Academy assholes jumped my brother.

"Mikey, you can't go doing this kind of shit! You gotta come to me first. Who were you going to fight with?" I asked, exasperated.

"Was gonna figure that out," he answered with a shrug. "You aren't around anymore, so you don't know how bad it's gotten for Mom. That asshole cuts her wages every week, and says she doesn't have enough business coming in. But she's not a demon! She doesn't have Burdock's connections."

Remorse flooded through me. I had no idea Lincoln killing Burdock would have such far-reaching consequences for my mom. Grim cut her wages every week? No wonder she'd rented out my room.

Oh God, now I was worried about my mom. Next paycheck, I was going to send her some money. If I had to, I'd force her to take it.

Shea's arm wrapped around Mikey's shoulders as she sat down. "Don't worry. Bri and I are going to win the money and get your mom out."

She was always so soft with him, cuddly. I just

usually socked him in the shoulder, and told him to shut up.

He looked up at me with a grin. "For real?"

I nodded. "When do registrations close?"

His long finger pointed to the fine print at the bottom of the flyer—the day of the Awakening.

We had time. I was sooo winning this fight.

——— · ———

After interrogating Mikey for every last scrap of info on this Fight Night, I informed him that he was now the new groundskeeper. At least for the summer.

Once he got over the fact that he was going to have to actually do work to earn his keep, we all settled into a nice flow. He did the grounds keeping, and Shea and I trained our asses off. I told Raphael about the Tainted Army thing, but he didn't seem surprised, only saddened.

Now we only had a few days left of summer, and the Awakening ceremony was tomorrow.

Shea stood in the gym, clutching her disc weapons, sweat dripping down her chest and a badass look in her eye. Lincoln stood before her with his blue fiery sword held aloft.

"Cut me!" he roared, and Shea advanced. Her fists held the flat grips of the blades while the sharp semicircles lashed out, seeking to cut my man. Lincoln was a blur, so fast I could barely track him.

He and the boys had been training us hard. As I was distracted watching them, Noah kicked out my feet and suddenly I was falling. Next thing I knew, his blade was at my neck.

Frick.

He looked down at me, sweat glistening against his perfect porcelain skin. "When fighting two on two, you need to keep your eye on your own fight. Getting distracted with what Shea's doing will only get you killed."

He was right. When the time came, I needed to just worry about my own fight.

With a rapid spin, I turned out of reach of his sword and used my legs to scissor-kick him. As I connected with his legs, he came tumbling down, and I grappled to gain leverage, moving on top of him. As I was crawling up his body, in an effort to straddle him and try to pin him down, his hand shot out, chopping me in the throat.

Holy shitballs.

Pain exploded in my neck as I fought to breathe. A lump had formed in my throat, and I'd keeled over to the side in a weak defense.

Noah looked sideways at me. "That was a dirty move, and I feel really bad for using it, but the Tainted Academy kids are going to fight dirty like that, so you need to be prepared."

With tears leaking out of the sides of my eyes, all I could do was nod. He was right. He was so right it hurt.

Lincoln and Shea had paused their fight and were taking a break.

"You're right," Lincoln said to Noah. "Which gives me an idea."

"Oh no. I don't like that face. You're doing *the* face," I told him.

He just grinned and then looked at Shea. "Okay, when are you calling him?"

Air blew through Shea's full lips. "I dunno. Now-ish."

We decided Shea would be the one to call Master Grim and ask his permission for us to enter Demon City to register for the fight contest, since I'd been the one to try and kill him and all.

Lincoln shook his head. "Okay, get three passes. I'm going with you girls."

A frown pulled at Noah's lips. "Hey, I've never been to Demon City. I want to go too."

Shea's conspiratorial look connected with his. "Trust me, you aren't missing anything."

"Just ask," Lincoln told her, holding out her phone.

She chewed her bottom lip. "Man, I feel sick. What if he says no? All this time will have been wasted."

"Don't let him say no. You know him. Use everything you got," I encouraged.

She took a deep breath and dialed his number on speakerphone, then started to pace.

"What do you want?!" he barked the second he picked up. She'd worked for him for six years, so of course he'd have her number saved in his phone.

Shea stopped in her tracks and rubbed her sweaty palm on her pants leg. "To give you a million bucks for Kate Atwater's demon contract," she replied, voice as smooth as butter.

Grim laughed good-naturedly. "Don't waste my time with fairy tales, angel lover," he spat.

My bestie chewed her lip. "I'm not. I just need you to get me four passes into Demon City so I can sign up for Fight Night. When my team wins, I'll give you the money. *All of it*. In return, you release Kate's contract."

Silence. Long-ass, terrifying silence. *Did he hang up?*

"You can't win. You've no doubt gotten weak in Angel City. Don't waste my time." Then he hung up.

He freaking hung up.

"Bastard!" Shea screamed at the phone, then sat down on the floor, and started typing furiously on the keyboard.

Frowning, I walked over. "What are you…?" My question faded when I noticed she'd pulled up Grim's picture from one of his strip club websites.

"I'll show him who's weak." She started to rock back and forth, chanting and moving her hands left

21

and right as dark blue magic leaked out, covering the phone.

"Is that light magic?" Lincoln's voice held concern.

I raised an eyebrow, but Shea ignored his question.

"It's make-his-horns-fall-off magic," she declared, and I blanched.

"Shea—" Before I could talk her off the ledge, the phone lit up with a call from Pansy-Ass Boss Man.

Shea stopped her magic and grinned, answering with a purr, "Why, hello there?"

"What are you doing?!" he roared. I could practically imagine the spittle flying from his mouth.

"Who's weak now?" Shea sneered into the phone. "Two months ago, I helped kill four demons, so don't tell me I can't win. That million bucks is *mine*," she growled.

Silence.

More silence.

"No, it's mine. You've got a deal. Now, stop fucking with my horns," he rumbled and hung up.

Shea smiled as we all looked at each other in shock and relief. Two minutes later, he texted her a one-hour travel pass for four people from Angel City.

"Let's ride," Lincoln called out.

CHAPTER 3

T HE NEXT DAY, WE SET OUT TO REGISTER FOR FIGHT Night. After getting past the border with our passes, Shea instructed Lincoln on how to get to Tainted Academy. The longer we drove, the more Noah and Lincoln shifted in their seats, looking uncomfortable.

"How come Shea and I don't feel like shit when we're here but you do?" I asked Lincoln.

He gave me a side glance. "Shea doesn't feel it because only Celestials do, and you don't because..." He eyed the mark on my chest.

Ah. Interesting. Because I wasn't a full-fledged Celestial, I was a Lucifer hybrid.

Ugh. Sorry I asked.

"Left down this alley," Shea added, leaning forward.

We careened between two brick buildings and down a skinny alleyway. When we reached the end, there was a black wrought-iron gate guarded by a demon slave who looked like a WWE wrestler. He was clutching a sleek black gun in his oversized left hand.

Lincoln rolled down the window and the guard glared at him, nostrils flaring.

"What are you doing here?" he spat.

Lincoln handed him his phone, which had the barcode showing we were approved to be in Demon City. "We're here to enroll in Fight Night," Lincoln told him.

The guard glanced at it and shrugged. "Says you can be in Demon City. Doesn't say I have to let you in Tainted Academy."

Dammit.

I was about to speak when Shea rolled down her window, directly behind Lincoln. The guard snapped his eyes in her direction.

"What's the matter, sugar tits? Afraid you'll lose to a couple Fallen Academy kids?" Shea questioned.

He glared at her, his eyebrows drawing together to form one bushy scowl. "You the one entering?"

"Me and my bestie," Shea answered with a nod, waving her thumb towards me. "Gonna wipe the floor with these Tainted Academy kids."

His glare turned to a grin and then a full-blown laugh. Reaching down, he pulled out his walkie-talkie. "I need an escort for some Fallen Academy douchebags. Keep your eye on the dark-haired one. He's one of the leaders of the Fallen Army."

He looked at Lincoln and winked, then slapped the hood of the car.

We drove on through, my man at the wheel, scowling.

Noah turned to Shea. "How did you know that would work?"

She smiled, shaking her head. "Please. Men are run by two things: their dick and their ego. Dick, ego, dick, ego—"

Noah waved a hand in her face, shutting her up. "Got it."

I chuckled and looked over at Lincoln, who was grimacing behind the steering wheel. "How did he know you?" I asked him.

He shook his head. "I've never seen that guy before in my life."

Noah leaned forward, popping his head between us. "Yeah, that was weird. We should tell Raph."

Lincoln just nodded and pulled into a parking spot near the entrance, where two large men were standing with automatic rifles.

"Shit, man, they're packing here. This is a school, right?" Lincoln leaned back to glance at Shea.

A dark look crossed her face and she nodded. "A messed-up school, yeah."

Now the guys were walking to our car. Lincoln opened the door and stood tall.

"No weapons on campus," the big brute with black bushy hair, and a red crescent moon tattoo on his forehead warned.

Lincoln was quiet for a whole forty-five seconds before he leaned into the car and whispered, "Noah, you stay here with the weapons. If I text you, drive onto campus and bring me my sword."

Holy shit, does he think we're going to have trouble?

Unstrapping his sword, he placed it on the center console.

Noah's gaze filled with longing while he focused on the campus. It was clear he wanted to see the inside, but he just nodded to Lincoln as Shea and I got out. I wasn't sure if they were going to check us, and I couldn't risk Sera getting taken, so I left her on the seat.

As I made my way around the car to stand next to Lincoln, I saw the men looking him over, checking him for weapons.

"What about him?" They pointed to Noah, who had crawled into the front seat.

"My driver isn't feeling well. He's going to stay in the car," Lincoln answered with a straight face.

It was clear Lincoln had been the one to drive us. The dark-haired demon slave scowled at him and then moved on to me. I was wearing pretty tight clothes, but he asked me to lift my shirt and spin around so he could check me for hidden weapons.

26

When I was completing my full spin, he let out a catcall whistle and stared at my abdomen.

Lincoln's wings snapped out and he stepped forward, no doubt ready to pummel the guy.

My hand shot out and I laid it on his chest. "Let it go," I murmured.

The demon slave was grinning ear to ear.

"You're next, sweetheart," the redhead told Shea.

Shea's resting bitch face was on as she lifted her shirt and did a spin.

"So, you girls think you can win in a fight against our best?" He looked Shea and me up and down.

Screw this guy. With little more than a thought, my wings snapped out, the tips now touching Lincoln's.

Their eyes widened at my black wings, and they seemed to just now notice the Prince of Darkness's tattoo on my chest.

Shea stepped forward. "You just show us where to sign up, sugar. That money is ours." She was the best at sweet-talking a guy down from a fight.

He grinned. "We'll see about that."

Lincoln was like an animal poised to attack. His entire body was tense and rigid, unmoving even to breathe. I knew if those guys even reached for a weapon, he'd grab Shea and me and fly us to Angel City.

The guys took one last look at Lincoln, rolled their eyes, and started walking to the entrance.

I stepped toward my man, slipping my hand into his, and tugged for him to follow. We needed to register for the fight or I couldn't save my mom.

Lincoln waited until our security detail was a good twenty feet ahead so they couldn't hear when he started talking shit.

"He looked at you like a piece of meat. I want to cut his eyes out," he growled.

My eyebrows hit my hairline. "Damn, who's the dark one now?"

"I told you this school was messed up. They'll probably let us sign up, and then as we're leaving, they'll jump us or some shit," Shea whispered.

Lincoln scoffed. "I'd like to see them try."

Shea and I shared a look. They had semiautomatic rifles. We were weaponless, *and* Lincoln wasn't looking so hot, sweating and breathing heavy. If they jumped us, we were getting our asses kicked for sure.

We entered the quad, and I could see right away that the buildings had fallen into disrepair. They were all cracked brick and corrugated metal of different colors, with two large buildings off to the left and a smaller strip of classrooms to the right. The campus must have been an old middle school or something. It was nothing grand like Fallen Academy.

Our guards had walked through the small atrium, and were now standing before an open classroom door.

As we approached, Lincoln stepped in front of

me and walked up to the door, peering in. The guys had to step out of the way to avoid his wings. Lincoln must have been satisfied with what he saw because he entered the room, his wings folding back to get through the door.

The guards scowled down at us as we followed him inside, Shea in front of me as I tucked my own wings back to fit.

My eyes fell to my watch. We were only permitted to be here for one hour. My gut told me if we overstayed our welcome, they had every right to do something about it. Now that Lincoln had moved out of the way, I could see a cheap card table had been set up with a hand-drawn poster in front. *Fight Night Sign-Ups* was scrawled across it in red paint that dripped to look like blood.

"I knew it would be you, Shelly." The girl who'd spoken sat behind the desk with a big hairy guy. She was staring at Shea.

Shea gritted her teeth, casting me a glance.

Damn, I wish I knew mind reading, because I had no idea who this bitch was.

The girl stood. She was tall with bright pink hair, and had the death mark tattoo on her wrist that marked her as a Dark Mage. "When they told me some prissy Fallen Academy kids wanted to sign up for Fight Night, I just knew it would be that bitch, Shelly." She winked.

Shea's breath was coming out in ragged gasps,

and I knew it was taking everything within her to not run over, and smack this girl down.

I stepped forward. "It's Shea, actually. And I'm Brielle. You might want to write that down so you spell it right on our million-dollar check."

She looked momentarily shocked at my words, but she smoothly covered it with a laugh and looked at her hairy boyfriend. "Oh my God, they are adorable. I can't wait to pulverize them."

At her last words, a blackish-green magic rose up from her hands and I froze.

Shea had seemed to find her Zen now, stepping forward and holding out her hand. In it was our entrance money. "So where do we sign?" Shea added, ignoring the sickly looking magic exuding from the girl's hands.

The magic retreated and the girl crossed her arms, looking at the one-hundred-dollar bill in Shea's hand.

"Oh, hun. That was the Tainted Academy price. If *you* want to enter, it's going to be a grand. Each." She grinned as her boyfriend laughed.

Bitch.

"We don't have that kind of money!" I shouted. This was all a shit show. They weren't even going to let us enter. How was I going to get my mom out of here now? We'd trained for nothing!

She shrugged. "Then run along, sweetie. Your boy toy isn't looking so hot."

I followed her gaze to Lincoln, who was grimacing, sweat rolling down his neck. I'd forgotten how badly being there affected him.

"Do you take Angel Express?" Lincoln asked and whipped out his credit card.

My eyes went wide, as did Pink Hair's.

"You really want a beatdown that badly?" she scoffed.

Shea and I nodded, which felt stupid considering what she'd just asked us.

"Fine. It's your funeral." Leaning forward, she snatched Lincoln's card, swiping it into an attachment on the end of her phone. She also had a little printer set up next to a cash box.

"I need to see ID," the boyfriend growled.

Shea and I stepped forward, pulling out our Angel City IDs, which showed our name, school address, and age.

He swiped them into some machine and it started printing.

My gaze went over to Lincoln, and he was signing his credit card receipt. I wanted to tell him not to, that I'd never be able to repay him *two grand*, but he just looked at me and winked.

Ah, the wink. *Sigh.* Wink number four. Each one was engraved in my heart. I was a sucker for Lincoln Grey's winks.

"Brielle Atwater," the hairy boyfriend said, looking at his girlfriend.

Her eyes narrowed on me, and then she grinned. "Mike's sister, I presume?"

In that instant, I saw red. If she said one more word about my brother, I was painting this room with her blood.

"Knock it off," Shea barked at her, snatching our IDs back from the hairy boyfriend.

She was trying to bait me into a fight. I knew that, and still I couldn't get myself to calm down.

The boyfriend handed us four shiny barcode tickets. "Each fighter gets to bring someone to claim the body," he stated as I tucked the tickets into my pocket.

"See you on Fight Night," the girl called with fists clenched.

Shea smirked. "I hope you're competing."

Pink Hair nodded, rolling out her wrists. "Luckily my hands have healed from her brother's face." She looked at me and smirked.

I'm going to jail for murder.

My wings snapped out, and with one gust I was airborne, and flying at her. Her face was about to get ripped off.

A sharp pain shot through my right wing, and I yelped as I was flung backward.

Lincoln.

Motherfu—

"She wants this! You're playing into her hand. Save it," he whispered.

The searing pain in my wing was throbbing as he kept an iron grip on it. I'd been thrown against his body, and he now had one hand wrapped around my waist as well.

The girl was grinning at me, blackish-green magic erupting from her palms once more. She was ready to throw down.

"Let's go," Shea snapped.

With another deep cleansing breath, I forced myself to walk away. I would save her ass-whooping for the ring. My eyes remained on hers while I allowed Lincoln to pull me away.

Payback was going to be a bitch.

We were escorted to the car quickly, where Noah sat anxiously behind the wheel. Once we were all inside—Shea and I in the back, with Lincoln up front—Noah started to drive home.

"How'd it go?" he asked. He looked like shit—sweaty, ashen, and he hadn't winked once the whole time we'd been in Demon City.

"Fine. They've enrolled," Lincoln told him.

"Um, not fine," I countered, leaning forward. "I can't believe you spent two grand on that. It'll take me two years to pay that back." Or more if I was going to be helping out my mom.

He chuckled, looking down at me. "You're welcome."

I groaned. "Well thank you, obviously, but I hope that didn't break the bank." I didn't know his financial situation, but living out of a trailer while the rest of the boys stayed in nice Fallen Army apartments didn't bode well.

Noah laughed. "Lincoln's rich. It's fine."

Lincoln cut him a glare.

"Oh," I murmured. "I assumed with the trailer…"

Noah busted out laughing. "I told you that trailer was ghetto."

Lincoln reached over and socked him in the arm. "I like my trailer." Then he turned to face me. "I'm not loaded, but my parents left some money behind with the life insurance so…yeah. I don't mind spending it on you girls."

Oh my God. He spent his parents' death money on me. Love exploded in my chest, and I vowed right then and there to one day have Lincoln Grey's babies.

Shea squeaked out an "aw," and I smiled.

"Who knew this entire time you were just a pretend asshole?" I stated.

A frown pulled at his lips. "Pretend asshole? Is that a thing?"

Leaning forward, I ran my fingers through his hair, pressing a kiss to his cheek. "It is."

"I think he's a real asshole who only has nice moments," Noah piped up.

Another sock in the arm.

"Oww."

Shea chuckled. "An asshole and a manwhore go on an adventure in Demon City. Sounds like the beginning of a messed-up children's book," she lamented.

Laughter erupted out of me as we reached the gates to Angel City.

Noah stopped the car when we reached traffic and looked over at Lincoln. "Can I be a manwhore if I haven't touched another woman besides Shea in almost a year?"

Lincoln grinned. "Nope. You can't."

They both looked back at Shea, who was glaring, but she just thrust her palm out in a 'talk to the hand' move. "Whatever."

The hard-to-get act was going to crash and burn soon. She needed to claim that shit, or Noah was going to walk.

But we had an Awakening ceremony to attend for my brother, so there was no sense in trying to fix her life now. That was going to have to wait.

CHAPTER 4

WHAT IF I HAVE BLACK WINGS LIKE YOU?" MY brother asked as we walked up to the Awakening ceremony.

My jaw went slack. I'd never thought of that. In all the scenarios I'd played through my head the past few hours, *that* had never occurred to me.

"Then we'll deal with it," I told him.

Please God, don't let him be like me. I couldn't handle Lucifer being after my brother too.

Lincoln and Shea were walking with us, and Lincoln put a hand on my brother's shoulder. "You're a free soul, so no matter what, you'll be at Fallen Academy with your sister. Nothing to worry about, bro."

Bro. Oh my God. My ovaries did somersaults at Lincoln's nice gesture toward my little brother.

Mikey grinned at him and nodded.

Shea tipped her chin down and chuckled a little. "Unless you're a Gristle. Then you're screwed and the academy won't want you."

I reached back and swatted her head.

"Kidding. You're going to be fine," she added, rubbing the spot I'd hit.

We finally reached the doors where the other kids were waiting to be let in. I knew the nerves Mikey must be feeling—hell, I'd felt them just the year before.

Leaning over, I gave my brother a tight hug. "Whatever it is will be fine. I love you," I told him.

He nodded curtly and waved to Lincoln and Shea before walking awkwardly to stand at the end of the line.

Lincoln was wearing his Fallen Army uniform. He was going to work the stage again, like he had with Raphael when I'd gone through my Awakening. It was reassuring to know that if anything went wrong, he'd be there to help my brother.

After making our way inside, we handed the attendant our tickets.

One of her eyebrows raised. "Front row. Fancy, fancy." She ripped the ticket, giving us the other half.

Front row! I hadn't even looked. Lincoln had given them to us. I glanced over at my boyfriend and he winked.

Ah, wink number five. Be still my heart.

"I'll see you after. Don't worry." He kissed me chastely.

As he walked away, Shea linked her arm with mine and dragged me toward the interior hall.

"Front row. Damn, girl, Lincoln loves you." She batted her eyelashes.

I smiled. "He does."

Front row was for Fallen Army officials, and rich families of kids who were going through the Awakening, not Lucifer's stepdaughter with the black wings.

I did a quick check to make sure my boots didn't have bloodstains on them. *Maybe I should have dressed nicer.*

"Sucks that your mom can't sit with us," Shea commented.

My heart pinched as a pang of sadness washed through me. I craned my neck to try to find her. There, in the nosebleed section with the other demon bound slaves she sat, looking tired as hell. I'd made an executive decision to not tell her about the whole fight thing, not yet.

She caught me looking and gave me a little wave. I waved back with a small smile.

"Please be seated, and we will bring out the students." Raphael's voice boomed from the stage.

Shea and I fast-walked to the front row and took our seats between some really important-looking people. One was an older dude wearing a Fallen

Army uniform with tons of medals on it, and the other was a lady with her hair so tight in a bun that it made her eyes pull up at the sides.

Shea and I tried to contain our giggles.

Oh my God, am I going to actually get to experience the after-party? The chocolate fountain and bliss donuts and all of the other things I never got to at my ceremony?

I looked up at the stage and tried to suppress my anger at seeing Grim and another demon there. His beady little eyes roamed over me, and then with a scowl, he turned away.

I should have killed him when I had the chance.

After a moment of sitting in the quiet, I heard the back doors open and everyone began to file in. Mikey looked super handsome in the black suit he wore. I gave him a thumbs-up and he rolled his eyes, red-faced and clearly embarrassed.

Whatever. I was a cool older sister.

Raphael gave his remorseful speech about the fallen war and infecting the humans with powers, and then he started to call the first name. Atwater would be one of the first.

Oh God, I was so nervous.

What if he was a Centaur? I'd never give him a hug without getting on a ladder first.

Shea must have known I was stressing, because she reached out and grasped my hand.

There was something so comforting about having

a best friend. Not just a bestie for a few years and then you grew apart. A. Best. Friend. Shea was stuck to me like glue, for life. No matter what, she was my person, and I was hers. Knowing we had each other, it took the weight off my shoulders in that moment. Whatever Mikey was, we would deal with it together.

"Melanie Anderson. Free soul," Raphael boomed, and I released the breath I'd been holding.

Being first sucked.

A waif-thin, timid-looking girl with mousy brown hair shuffled to the stage, her chin down. When she stood before Raphael, he beamed at her and held his hands over her head. A fine sprinkling of gold dust fell into her skin and we all froze. Even though she wasn't my family, I felt myself go rigid with anticipation. It was like watching a suspenseful movie.

Suddenly she began to cry, staring at her hands.

"No!" she shouted.

Raphael's upper lip curled, and Lincoln, who stood behind him, discretely covered his nose.

"Melanie Anderson. Gristle."

Oh shit.

I wasn't a pro lip reader, but I thought Raphael muttered, "I'm sorry," before she ran offstage crying.

Craning my neck back, I could see that my brother was as white as a sheet.

"Michael Atwater. Free soul," Raphael said next.

I hadn't expected the pang of pride that would swell in my chest when Raphael said "free soul" after my brother's name, but there it was. My mother and I had made some mistakes, but Mikey was a clean slate.

Shea squeezed my hand, and I squeezed back.

Damn, going after a Gristle reveal was a hard act to follow.

"You got this, Mikey!" Shea called out like a loud New Yorker.

I flinched as the snooty people next to us scowled down their noses at us, but it had worked. Mikey smiled shyly, and the color came back in his cheeks.

Okay. Breathe. Just breathe. God, please don't let him have black wings, or be a Centaur.

By the time I'd gotten out of my head, and focused on what was happening, Raphael had already started to drop the magic reveal dust or whatever it was.

Mikey just stood there, hands fisted and eyes forward. Terrified.

'*Poor lad,*' Sera said from my boot.

'*You scared me!*' I told her. I'd forgotten she was there.

'*Sorry,*' she whispered and then went quiet.

I was staring at my brother, waiting for something to happen, but nothing did. Raphael had finished sprinkling the dust, and now just stood in front of him watching, same with Lincoln.

Oh God. He's a dud. A freaking worthless human!

He'd get no admission to Fallen Academy, no job

41

with the Fallen Army, and would be homeless. Tears welled in my eyes, and Shea clenched my hand tight enough to hurt.

At that moment, a howl ripped from Mikey's throat and he lurched forward on all fours, panting in pain. The hairs on my arms shot up, and I leaned forward in my seat.

That howl wasn't human.

"Mikey?" I stood, brushing Shea's hand off.

His body was contorting, and the sound of cracking bones was so familiar to me that I actually felt some relief, and sat back down.

He was a Beast Shifter, like Luke. I could handle that. That was okay with me.

I glanced at Shea, who was smiling in relief as well.

My brother's suit tore as his body bulked out, black fur popping up everywhere, muscles stacking up over his form, and enlarging his mass. Beast Shifters were usually animals—deer, bears, mountain lions, and so on, whatever animal had been in the vicinity when the fall happened—and then they had horns, which gave them a demon look. Luke would be able to help Mikey through what shifting was like, and everything associated with being a Beast Shifter. I was actually okay with it. It felt right.

At least it did until my brother turned into a huge black wolf with black velvet horns, and searing yellow eyes. He looked freaking possessed as he bent down low, and started to growl at Raphael.

The archangel went stiff, and Lincoln slowly pulled his sword.

What the hell!

"Call Clark!" Lincoln barked to someone offstage, and the whole crowd gasped as Mikey lunged for Raphael.

Shooting out of my seat, I barreled towards the stage within seconds.

"Mikey, no!" I shouted, but it was too late. Raphael was forced to grab Mikey's shoulders and slam him to the ground in self-defense.

Lincoln held his sword aloft; it was glowing blue, and my brother was staring at it with a venomous gaze. His lips peeled back and he growled from his place, pinned on the floor beneath Raphael.

What the hell is happening? That was *not* my brother. I knew Lincoln wouldn't hurt him, but why the hell was he holding his sword at him?

I climbed onto the stage, and Lincoln's gaze shifted to me. "What's wrong?" I asked in a low voice.

Raphael still had my brother pinned, and I could tell it was taking great effort. His arms shook as the muscles flexed. My brother jerked, trying to slip free, but Raphael laid more of his weight on him and strengthened his hold.

Lincoln looked out over the crowd and kept his voice low. "He's a pack animal. When pack animals

43

shift for the first time, they're consumed with the need to hunt. He'll wipe out half this crowd if we can't get an alpha here soon."

What. The. Fuck.

I swayed on my feet, looking down at my little brother. He was *huge*, almost as big as Luke's bear, and it was clear now that Raphael was using all of his angelic strength to hold him.

An oversized wolf with demonic powers that wants to hunt humans. Awesome.

"Mikey?" I knelt down and tried to meet his eyes.

The growl that ripped from his throat, as he jerked his head in my direction, had tears lining my eyes. He'd wriggled his head free from Raphael, and was now snapping his teeth in my direction like a rabid dog.

"I can't hold him much longer." Raphael confessed through gritted teeth.

Oh. My. God.

'Pull me out,' Sera instructed.

'*What? No way. I'm not hurting my brother.*'

'*Pull me out. We won't seriously hurt him, but we might have to keep him from mauling the crowd,*' she told me.

I pulled Sera out, and Lincoln dropped his sword. He wrestled onto Mikey's back half, trying to hold him down. Raphael was becoming weaker; every time my brother thrashed, he gained more way.

"Where's Clark?!" Lincoln roared to someone

offstage. I kept my eyes on my brother, while I wondered who the hell this Clark guy was.

"He's coming!" a voice called back.

Mikey ripped free then. In one thrust, he rolled out of Raphael's and Lincoln's grasps, and then stood with his back to the demons, who'd been watching keenly the entire time.

"Evacuate the building," Lincoln ordered a Fallen Army guard, who was standing offstage with a gun in his hand.

"We'll take him off your hands," the demon sitting with Grim informed us, winking.

"Screw you," I snapped at the ugly demon.

Mikey had his head down and was glaring at me with those freaky yellow eyes.

"Mikey. It's me, Bri," I told him.

Movement to my left pulled my attention, but not enough to take my eyes off my brother.

"I can stun him if he lunges. It'll wear off quick, but it might help in the short run," Shea said as magic crackled at her palms.

I was trying to keep the tears at bay. My poor brother had been taken over by a monster.

'Let her,' Sera instructed me.

Turning my head slightly to my best friend, I nodded to Shea.

An Abrus demon I didn't know stepped closer. "He could learn more about his powers at Tainted Academy," he cooed.

I pivoted my body to him, Sera raised and glowing in my hand. "I will cut you if you go near my brother."

The demon scowled at me and took a step closer as if to threaten me.

I'd never seen Raphael with a weapon until right then. He tore across the space, blindingly fast, with a twelve-inch golden dagger in his hands. His wings flapped earnestly, causing a gust of wind to pick up my hair.

"He's a free soul. And free souls are *mine* to protect." Raphael's voice was so deep and menacing that I barely recognized it.

The demon cowed, taking a step back with his head lowered, and that's when Mikey lunged. Not for me, or Raphael, but for the demon.

Without uttering a word, Shea threw an orange fiery ball at Mikey's right shoulder. My brother howled as if in pain, hitting the ground. Limp. He'd dropped twelve inches from the Abrus demon.

"Shea!" I snapped.

"It's just a stun spell. He'll be—" She didn't finish her sentence because Mikey stood once more, a bit wobbly, and shaking his head as if to clear his thoughts.

Shit.

I really, really, *really* didn't want to kick my brother's ass.

"If he lunges for me again, I'm putting him

46

down!" the demon roared, smoke billowing from his ears.

I took one step into the demons' black-tiled side of the stage, and Sera pulsed a bright white light from her blade, sharp and quick. "Touch my brother and I will end your life!" My wings popped out of my back, and I heard some in the crowd gasp.

The demon's gaze went to my chest, and upon seeing the symbol there, he grinned. "You've got Lucifer's temper."

The comment was like a kick to the stomach. Did I? Was I like Lucifer?

I staggered backward and lowered my dagger slightly.

Mikey growled again and lowered his front end, sticking his hind legs into the air, preparing to pounce.

"Freeze!" a deep male voice boomed behind me. Mikey whined, lowering his bottom half, and going fully flat onto the ground.

I spun around to see a tall man in his early thirties leap onto the stage. His hair was chocolate brown, and fell in wild wisps around his face. He was stacked with muscles, like a linebacker, and his eyes were...haunting. They glowed an eerie honey color. He kept his eyes on my brother with each step he took.

This must be Clark.

"That's my brother," I told him. "Can you help him?"

He didn't take his eyes off Mikey. "That's up to him."

The alpha moved within a few feet from Mikey and my brother started to growl. Towering over him, Clark crossed his arms, and leaned forward. "Submit," he growled in a voice that was only half human.

Mikey's lips peeled back as his growl grew louder and he held the alpha's gaze.

Oh God. What does this mean?

Clark bent on one knee, shoving his face right in my brother's, and I stopped breathing.

"You *will* submit to me, or I cannot help you," he declared.

Holy shit. My brother was going to rip his face off. I was sure of it.

A few more seconds into the stare-down and Mikey's growl turned to a whine, his amber eyes falling to Clark's shoes. Then my brother lowered his head and rolled onto his back, exposing his belly.

Clark's meaty hand reached out and grabbed the scruff of my brother's neck, shaking it. "Good pup. Let's go," he barked and stood.

"What? Where are you going?" My voice trembled as Mikey rose to a standing position and stood at Clark's side.

Clark's honey-colored eyes flicked to me for the first time, and I felt a physical power wash over me.

"I'm taking him to my land. I'll teach him to hunt deer and calm his thirst for the kill. When I'm satisfied he won't hurt a human, I'll send him to school," the alpha declared.

Umm, what the hell did he just say?

"Can't you just force him to change back to human? Then he won't hurt anyone." Right? I was kicking myself for not paying much attention, during the week we spoke about Beast Shifters in my fallen history class. I figured everyone was like Luke—shift, kick some demon ass, shift back.

Clark shook his head. "He won't be able to change back until he's quenched his thirst for the hunt."

A strangled gasp reached us, and I turned to see my mother listening in on our conversation.

Oh great.

"Well, can I visit him?" I called out. He was walking away with my brother on his heels.

"Maybe," he called back.

My eyes flew to Lincoln, who just shrugged.

There was a cluster of men and women waiting by the door for Clark. When he neared, they bowed their heads, and stepped out of the way to let him pass. After he and my brother were out of sight, they pulled in the rear and left behind him. They were like a freaking cult.

'Or a wolf pack,' Sera offered.

I didn't need a dose of her logic right then. My heart was hammering in my chest.

49

"Well, that wasn't ideal, but Clark will take good care of him," Raphael offered.

The archangel was standing now, dagger sheathed, and wings down calmly at his sides.

What a crazy day.

But 'not ideal'?

My brother was stuck as a monster, and had just gone to live with some dude I'd never heard of for God knew how long.

"Extremely *not* ideal," I told him, then went to comfort my mother.

If life would stop shitting on me, that would be great.

CHAPTER 5

I'D LEFT THE AWAKENING CEREMONY EARLY TO drive my mom back, and assure her that I would take care of Mikey. That this Clark guy was someone we could trust, and everything would be okay. Lincoln told me to let myself into his trailer and wait for him, that he'd wrap up his duties at the ceremony and meet me there.

I let myself in, and after fifteen minutes I was bored off my ass.

'Let's snoop,' Sera offered.

I chuckled. '*Oh my God, how are you an angel's blade?*'

'*Good question. They probably messed up when they made me. That's why I got sent to Earth.*'

My chest vibrated as I laughed again. '*Wait,

are you saying I'm only worthy of a reject infinity weapon?'

'Did you just call me a reject?' she retorted.

A grin lit up my face and momentarily all of my worries washed away.

'What's that little poetry book?' Sera pressed.

My eyes flicked to the brown leather-bound book in front of me and I shook my head.

'No way. That's messed up,' I told my blade.

'They're just poems. It's not like a journal,' Sera pressed harder.

I groaned. *'Fine, one look. Because I'm bored and curious what he writes in there.'*

On nights that I studied over there, he would scribble in the book and play his guitar.

Reaching over, I flipped through the pages to the last, most recent one.

Eyes like the sky, they behold mighty power.
Hair like the sun, I want to stay warm forever.
Her love fills me up, fills me up—

The door handle jiggled and I chucked the book across the table. It slammed against the wall and fell awkwardly onto the bench seat.

"Hey," Lincoln said as he walked in.

"Nothing," I shouted.

Oh God, that song sounded like it was about me. My cheeks reddened.

'What a sweetheart,' Sera cooed.

"Are you okay?" Lincoln frowned, moving

toward me. I scooched over to give him room to sit next to me.

"Yep, fine. Up to nothing." I laughed nervously.

Lincoln's brows drew together. "I mean about your brother. Are you okay?"

In my snoop-fest, I'd momentarily forgotten about my brother. "Oh. No, I'm not okay about that. He must be so scared, and I don't know that Clark guy, but he seemed like a dick. My mom was totally freaking out too."

Lincoln rubbed my back slowly, up and down, over and over as I vented everything that was bothering me.

"I just want a freaking break, ya know!" I shouted. "First I have black wings, then this crazy prophecy that I'm going to kill Lucifer, and my devil mark tattoo. I thought that was enough to deal with."

He nodded in understanding. "It is enough. More than enough. But we'll get through this together."

"Now my brother told me that my mom's boss is docking her pay every week, and I'm afraid she's not even getting enough to eat. She would never tell me if she was struggling that hard."

Lincoln frowned. "I have ten grand left of my parents' insurance policy money. She can have it if she needs it."

My chest shuttered with emotion. *Who is this amazing man, and how the hell do I deserve him?*

53

"No, I'm going to send her some money out of my monthly checks. But Lincoln... Wow. Thank you for offering."

He was staring at me with those intense blue eyes, messy dark hair, and pouty full lips, and all of a sudden my mind was off my troubles, and on the man candy before me.

He must have noticed the moment my mood shifted, because he looked down at my lips then back up at me with a half-lidded gaze.

"I love you," I whispered tenderly, leaning forward to brush my lips across his.

His hand came up to thread into my hair as he gripped the back of my neck. Our kiss grew deeper as heat pooled in my gut. I'd never been so sexually attracted to someone as I was to Lincoln. Just the way he looked at me behind those dark lashes, with those moistened lips, it undid me.

I stood and grabbed my lower back. "I've really had this kink in my back lately. I'd love a back rub."

He smirked, looking me up and down. "If you want to have sex with me, just say it."

Laughter pealed out of me. "I totally want to have sex with you."

'Get a room.' Sera's voice invaded my mind.

Ignoring her snarky comment, I pulled her out of my leg harness and set her next to Lincoln's sword.

Lincoln's strong hands came around to cup my

butt as he lifted me up to straddle him. I pressed my thighs around his waist to keep myself on him and pulled off my shirt. His eyes fell to the tattoo on my chest before he bent forward and kissed it. Every time he did that, it made me emotional, and a lump formed in my throat. It was like he was saying he approved of me, all of me, and he loved every part of me. Even the less desirable ones.

We'd made it to the bed and fell into it together. Lincoln pulled off his shirt in one of those sexy one-handed moves and pressed his pelvis against me. I moaned and gripped the back of his neck, peppering his shoulder with kisses as he started to unbutton my pants.

"School starts tomorrow," I huffed, panting. "You know what that means?"

His eyes were practically glowing as he looked up at me from kissing my belly button.

"What?"

I grinned. "I don't have to call you 'sir' anymore."

The grin was wiped off my face and exploded into a moan as he worked his tongue magic. I'd call him 'sir' for the rest of my life as long as he kept doing that.

———◆·◆———

"Thank you for seeing me, Brielle." Mr. Claymore motioned me to step into his office.

"Are you kidding? When I got your message, I was so excited I barely slept."

We were only a few days into school, and he thought he'd found a spell that could remove my devil mark. Setting my bag on the floor, I took a seat in a chair across from his desk. Class started in forty-five minutes, but I'd willingly gotten up at six thirty to be ready for this.

He smiled, and I couldn't help but notice how kind his eyes were. Other than the streaks of gray in his brown hair, you wouldn't know he was an older man.

"Now, I want to warn you, this may not work. So don't get your hopes up." Pulling off his thick black cloak, he laid it over his chair and rolled up his sleeves.

I nodded. "Got it. Totally not overexcited or anything." I bopped in my seat, trying to hide my grin.

He chuckled. "Come in!"

A frown pulled at my lips, not having heard anyone knock, and I was surprised to see Raphael step into the room, tucking his wings back as far as he could to squeeze into the space.

"Hello, Brielle." His voice was always so calm.

"Hey. Wasn't expecting to see you here."

He made his way behind Mr. Claymore's desk, and looked up at me with his piercing blue eyes. The way his golden blond hair glowed around his shoulders, sort of reminded me of the halos Catholics always depicted around the angels' heads. "Oh, I'm just here to drop a little Celestial magic and leave. What you two do with it is none of my concern."

He winked just as his hands suddenly glowed with a crazy bright orange healing light, so bright, I had to shield my eyes. I peeked back over to the desk, through my fingers, to see him pouring the golden light into a large jar. Once it was full, he nodded to Mr. Claymore, and moved back around the desk to the door.

"Have a good day," he offered cheerfully, and then he left.

I busted out laughing. "That was super shady."

Mr. Claymore chuckled softly, but then his face fell into a more stoic pose. "Raphael cannot directly help the humans, so he does what he can in obscure ways."

My lips turned down into a frown. "Why not? What would happen if he did?"

Mr. Claymore put on a pair of thick leather gloves. "If he does...he can't go home."

Home?

'*Heaven, you dingbat,*' Sera barked.

'*Oh shit.*'

"Oh. Why?" I was totally prying, but I needed to know everything about this.

The Light Mage picked up the jar with his thick leather gloves and sighed. "It's just his penance, that's all. Don't worry. Now, this might hurt a bit, so take a deep breath."

Raphael's penance for what?

He was standing over me now, holding the glowing jar of Raphael's magic, his own purple light beginning to sneak in and mix. I wasn't sure if I was supposed to drink it or what, until he upended it right onto my bare chest and a burning sizzle erupted across my flesh.

I hissed, as the golden purplish light saturated my chest, and sank into the skin there. Then, a cool minty feeling spread across it.

"Sorry," he mumbled.

I nodded, breathing in and out heavily, looking down at the tattoo that was still very much there. My skin was starting to turn an angry red, and the burning was back. Mr. Claymore began to chant, sprinkling clumps of salt down my shirt.

I was just starting to think this was going to work when movement to my left caught my eye. My head snapped to the side, and my mouth dropped at the portal that was slowly opening in the middle of the air.

"Uhhh," I said, and pointed.

The Light Mage looked back at the portal and cursed, nearly dropping an entire bottle of salt on me.

"Get behind me," he muttered.

Oh shit. Why can't anything go my way?

I stood, pulling Sera out, and stepped behind the professor.

The portal grew wider and a dilapidated stone building came into view. The building didn't scare me, but the stench of sulfur did.

"Is… Is that Hell?" I gasped.

He was throwing streaks of purple across the room, which were attaching to the edges of the portal and forcing it closed.

My chest no longer burned, or felt cool, or felt… anything. I looked down, and other than a few grains of salt, it looked normal. The menacing skull with wings and a lopsided crown was still there, staring up at me.

My eyes flicked back up to see Mr. Claymore wrestling a tiny Yew demon that was trying to fly into the room with its little bat-like wings. It appeared as though Mr. Claymore had magically bound its mouth. Purple energy bands wrapped around it like the rubber bands they put around lobster claws. That was a good thing considering they spit fire.

'Stop horsing around and point me at him,' Sera demanded.

Oh. Right.

I tipped the blade over Mr. Claymore's shoulder and pointed the tip right at the Yew demon. A bright shot of white light erupted from the blade and slammed into its chest, knocking it backward. Mr. Claymore pulled tightly on the purple bands and the portal sealed shut.

Once he was satisfied it was closed, the Light Mage spun around and looked at Sera in my hand.

"Thanks for that." He nodded. His hair was a mess, completely wind-blown.

I just bobbed my head. "That was a portal to Hell," I stated matter-of-factly.

He looked down at my chest and frowned. "Brielle, I'm very sorry I wasn't able to remove your mark. It looks as though the Dark Prince has...a security system of sorts on it."

My gut tightened with fear. "You mean... You tried to take it off and..." I couldn't say it.

He looked utterly gutted. "And it opened the portal, which means I won't be able to remove it. I'm truly sorry."

A mental fog rolled over me, bringing with it a deep depression. I'd been totally stoked that I was going to be rid of the mark. I'd even told Lincoln and Shea to get ready to throw a party for me if it worked.

"I'm glad we didn't trigger the demon alarm. I'm sorry to have gotten your hopes up." Now he seemed to be taking all of the responsibility on himself. I wasn't about to let that happen.

I plastered on a fake smile. "Hey, it's all right. It doesn't hurt or anything. I'll be okay." I grabbed my bag and shouldered it.

"Go in peace," he whispered.

I left the room to find Shea and Lincoln across the hall, waiting expectantly. One look at my chest and their faces fell.

Go in peace, I did not.

CHAPTER 6

THE FIRST TWO WEEKS OF SCHOOL PASSED PRETTY smoothly. I had pretty much the same classes as last year, but instead of two hours with my Celestial master teachers, I had only one hour—alternating with the boys—and I had a new class called war strategies.

My brother was still in his wolf form and living with Clark on his land, which was God knew where. I'd called to check on him a few times, and they'd been brief thirty-second conversations where Clark informed me that Mikey was progressing fine, and then was silent to the point of awkward.

My mom was absolutely freaking out. Mikey was the baby of the family, and she just couldn't take it. She texted me daily, asking if I'd heard anything. I'd started lying and giving her more information than I'd received, like he was doing so well that he was no longer needing to hunt, he'd made friends, and he'd be human again soon. None of that was true, of course, but I would say anything to give her peace.

"Okay, it's almost done," Shea announced.

Chloe, Luke, Angela, and I were all huddled around Shea's desk in our dorm room. She was finally brewing Tiffany's payback potion.

"Is this going to throw her in the healing clinic?" I asked.

Shea nodded. "It better. Bitch nearly made us all fail by taking out Luke."

If she went to the healing clinic, she might rat us out. We were Fallen Army soldiers now and had signed a code of conduct form on the first day. I was guessing this was against the 'respecting fellow Fallen Army soldiers' bit.

"Is there any way one of the Mage teachers could trace this back to you?"

Shea looked off to the side of the room, seemingly lost in thought. "Good idea. I'll do a scent masking spell on top of it." She reached for a few jars of powdered God knew what, and threw a pinch in the potion.

"Whatever. Even if we get two weeks' detention, it'll be worth it," Chloe proclaimed.

We were all fond of shit-talking Tiffany—it's what had brought us closer. I just wanted to make sure I could keep my cushy job, now that I had my mom and brother to worry about.

I pulled out my phone and texted Lincoln.

Brielle: Hypothetically, if we spelled Tiffany to shit her brains out as payback and got caught...

His reply was immediate.

Lincoln: Delete this text, dummy. You'll get a week's community service.

Community service didn't sound so bad. I deleted the text and then looked at Shea. "Let's do it."

Shea grinned before snapping her fingers, and the potion puffed into purple smoke. Reaching in, she pulled out a small blue wafer-thin piece of paper.

Luke held out his hand. "I will have the honors."

Shea dropped the wafer on to his palm. "Just slip it in her drink or on her food. It'll dissolve and do the trick."

He gave a mischievous grin and nodded his head. "I've waited months for this day. You distract her," he told us, closing his meaty hand lightly around it.

We nodded.

Operation Make Tiffany Crap Her Brains Out was in full effect.

---•---

It wasn't too hard to slip her the spell—we just asked her questions about herself and she blabbered for ten minutes, then dismissed us like cattle. Now we were sitting at our table on the demon-gifted side of the dining hall, watching her intently. With every bite of soup she took, Luke grinned wider and wider.

"How many months until Fight Night?" he asked, never taking an eye off his prey.

"Six more. Lincoln's upped our training to insane levels." I groaned at the thought, but I was definitely going to be a well-trained assassin by the time we were done with all of it.

Shea rolled her neck; she'd mentioned it was kinked the day before. "Yeah, Noah's riding me hard." The second the words left her lips, her face took on a bright red hue. "I meant in training."

We all busted out laughing. Their Wednesday make-out sessions in his car had turned into "movie nights" at his place.

"Have you slept with him yet? I hear he's amazing." Chloe took a bite of her apple.

Shea grimaced. "No, and for the exact reason you just said. I'm not letting that dirty car park in my pristine garage."

Her garage was hardly pristine, but thank God we weren't saying 'wee wee' anymore. We'd finally grown to adult metaphors, and I couldn't be prouder.

"Oh come on, that's not what I meant," Chloe said, looking regretful.

Is now a good time to drop the truth bomb on my bestie? Probably not, but here goes.

"He totally, genuinely, cares for you, Shea. Loves you, even. If you don't reciprocate that—and I don't mean sexually, but emotionally—he'll leave."

Shea shot me full of ice daggers, and opened her mouth to speak when Tiffany shot out of her seat, clutching her stomach.

"You bitches!" she shouted across the hall at us, clenching her butt cheeks.

We all burst into fits of laughter as she ran out of the room. I laughed so long I was starting to worry I might actually piss myself.

"Revenge feels good. Next time, let's replace her toilet paper with sandpaper," Luke declared.

When I could finally breathe, I held my hands up. "There will be no next time. We got her back. Now we need to focus on school."

The last thing we needed was a raging Tiffany prank war.

Luke rolled his eyes. "Yes, Mom."

I blew him an air kiss, and focused on his sister instead.

"Angela, this weekend is our first Fallen Army gig. Can you tell us what they'll have us do, or are you magically gagged?" I asked, the fourth year.

Angela leaned forward, looking each of us in the eye. "The first time you go out, it's just to get you used to the outside war zones. Desensitize you, so to speak." A dark look crossed over her face, and she swallowed thickly. "But as the months drag on, you'll start to do missions," she confessed.

I stared at her with rapt attention. She was gone a few weekends last year, but I'd never thought anything of it, and when she got back, she never spoke about it. She'd said she helped the Fallen Army out a bit, but she'd never said that the gauntlet was their admissions tool. Now that I knew everything, I was seeing those missing weekends in a whole new light.

"What kind of missions? Girl, you can't leave it at that," Shea pressed her, putting extra sass into the word 'girl.'

"Most of it is just bringing aid to those who are trapped out there, food and water and stuff. Sometimes we've smuggled people out of hot zones, or fought down some serious baddies."

My breathing slowed. "Hot zones?"

She nodded, looking dejected. "Places where the demons have...captured humans, and other free souls."

Captured. She said captured.

"But they only ask for help with those missions from upperclassmen, third and fourth years. Only one time my second year, when they got low on soldiers, they asked us to help," she amended.

Chloe took a sip of her water, brushing back a chunk of her bright red hair that had popped out from behind her hood. "I can't wait to be a badass fourth year, ferrying free souls across the hot zones and into Angel City."

Luke laughed. "You have a hero complex."

She shrugged. "So what?"

Shea held up her hands. "All I care about right now is that Tiffany is stuck on a toilet somewhere."

As I laughed, I looked around at my friends. I'd totally grown attached to this crew and to my new life. Worry for Mikey and my mom, and the fact that this devil mark was permanent nagged at my insides, but overall, I was counting my blessings.

———•———

After all the fuss we'd made, Tiffany never ratted us out. It might have helped that Shea slid a note under her door that read, *snitches get stitches* in red paint that looked like blood, but the fact that she didn't tell on us actually scared me a little. Was she plotting revenge? Either way, we'd made it through the week, and were now minutes from leaving on our first weekend out in the war zone as Fallen Army reserve soldiers.

"Got you a present," Lincoln told me as we stepped out of his trailer. He had somehow snuck a box into his hands that I hadn't seen before.

"A prezzie? For me?" I spun, and ripped the shoe box out of his hands. It wasn't wrapped, which was so Lincoln. But he'd put my name on the top in pen with a small heart to dot the i. Again, so Lincoln. He was super romantic without trying too hard.

We hadn't really gotten each other presents before. For my last birthday, he'd bought Shea and me dinner. Then for Christmas, he got me a glitter unicorn phone case, and drew black angel wings onto the horse with a Sharpie. I'd gotten him guitar picks.

"Eager much?" he laughed, as I ripped the lid off without fanfare.

When my eyes fell on the steel cuffs, I gasped. "Are these…?"

"Custom battle cuffs. Made with the same stuff as our shield armor, so you can stop a sword with them if you need to," he confirmed.

My heart thumped wildly in my chest as I gazed at the man before me. Lincoln was my family. He'd lost his family, and moved out into this lonely trailer, until I shoved my way into his life. Now here we were. Whether he liked it or not, he was stuck with me.

"I'm going to marry you one day," I said suddenly, then winked to make it more lighthearted than I truly meant it. But seriously, I needed to lock this dude down before he realized he could probably do better.

"Hey, I'm supposed to be saying those things," he answered with a grin.

I scoffed. "Don't be sexist."

He rolled his eyes. "Woman, try them on. Do you have any idea how hard it is to measure your arms while you're sleeping? You shove them between your legs!"

My laughter rang out, filling the air around us as I popped on my tiptoes to plant a kiss on his lips.

My mom told me once that your first love was dangerous. First love could make you, but also destroy you. If Lincoln was to be my destroyer, I was okay with that—it was worth the making of me.

I finally reached in and pulled the cuffs out, letting the box fall to my feet. Tilting my arm to the side, I slipped the cuff over it and then straightened it so it fit neatly in place.

"Like a glove," I told him.

They were exquisite. The front had an engraved pair of angel wings on each cuff, with my name underneath. They shined in the sunlight, showcasing their fresh silver polish.

"They should save your ass on Fight Night." He ran a hand through his hair, smoothed his shirt, and tucked it into his pants. We'd totally just had a quickie in his trailer, so he was trying to tuck in his uniform, hiding the evidence.

I smoothed my hair as well. "So, third year I get to move into the Fallen Army barracks, and I can keep those living quarters even after graduation?" I asked. I'd read the salary package with an eagle eye. Mostly because it was the best job I'd ever had, and I was going to need to take care of my mom and Mikey.

He ran a hand down the side of his trailer, looking at it fondly. "Yeah. Some students like to stay in the dorms if they have younger siblings there, like Angela and Luke, or you and your brother. I used to share an apartment in the barracks with Noah, but..."

I knew this shit was painful for him to talk about, but I wanted to know everything about him. Like why he was the only guy who lived on campus in a trailer.

"After my family died, I didn't want to step foot in our family home. It was like a memory crypt. But this was our camping trailer. Just enough good memories that it wasn't overwhelming."

Oh God, I felt bad for asking.

I placed my hand over his. "It's a pretty sweet little pad," I told him.

He smiled, looking down at me with those crystalline blue eyes. Visually, Lincoln and I were opposites. Where my hair was blonde, his was dark; where my wings were black, his were white. But we couldn't be more perfect for each other. When I didn't want to kill him, I was madly in love with him. That was the most anyone could ask for, right?

He stroked my hair and tucked it behind my ear. "My mom would have loved you. She always told

70

me, 'Don't settle. Wait for a strong woman and she'll raise strong daughters.' You're the strongest person I know, Brielle."

My heart melted at the compliment, and my stomach did flip-flops at his reference to his mother's approval of me. He barely talked about his late parents, and never about his little sister, so it meant even more that he'd shared that part of himself.

"She was kind of a raging feminist." He laughed, seemingly lost in the memory.

"Sounds like a smart woman. How did your dad keep her locked down?" I joked.

A genuine and open smile stretched Lincoln's lips, one I'd never seen before. "He didn't. Said that was his secret. Never try to cage the free bird." He winked.

I'd officially lost count of how many winks he'd given me.

I wished I could have met his parents. Lincoln had only met my mom a few times when she'd come to visit, and while he was polite, I knew his cautious glances at her forehead meant he'd never fully trust her. Not until I could free her.

Before I could say something sickeningly lovey-dovey, the walkie-talkie on his belt loop squawked.

"Grey, you coming?" Noah urged through the device.

Lincoln smoothed his hair one last time, then leaned forward, and kissed me chastely. "See you soon. You're on my team tonight," he declared before he started to jog away.

"Do I have to call you, sir?" I screamed after him.

"Yes!" he yelled, and then he was gone.

Dammit. He was going to milk this 'sir' thing for a while.

I ran my fingers along the wing engravings on the cuffs and smiled.

We could pretend all day that he was in charge, but I knew the truth.

CHAPTER 7

S HEA'S FACE WAS PRESSED AGAINST THE GLASS, looking out the window as we left Angel City, and made our way into the war zone.

"Tonight is just a drive-by. We want you to see what we're up against, and get a sense for the terrain. To hear the noises, see the risks, and then come right back," Lincoln told us as he paced the aisle, holding onto the handrail above him intermittently. "You're rookies. You won't be doing missions for a while, so don't ask," he barked to our small group of nine second-year rookies and Noah, plus the driver.

Luke raised his hand. "So people, like, live out here? Why don't we just ferry them into Angel City by the busload?"

Lincoln's face took on a hardened expression.

"Unfortunately it's not that easy. A lot of the people out here are slave bound. Those who aren't are trapped in some kind of deal with a demon that keeps them here. The demons out here run the war zones like a mafia. If you live in their territory, you have to pay protection money."

"Oh," Luke said and looked out at the desolate landscape. We were passing the area we'd done the gauntlet in. The broken-down neighborhoods and shelled-out buildings, some still smoldering, were depressing to say the least.

"Another issue is resources," Lincoln continued. "Angel City is only so big, and we only have so much to go around. The demons outnumber us greatly, and they've taken so much of our land. We try to push back and take back certain parts, but when we finally do, they look like this." He gestured to the windows.

Geez, I was very fortunate to be living in Angel City. They didn't cover the war on the news or anything like that. The news was still run by the humans, and they mostly talked about things going on in Angel City, with an occasional story about Demon City, or beyond the wall. I'd never seen a news crew out here, or heard a Fallen Army soldier interviewed. We knew the war with the demons was ongoing, but we were safe in our little city and we had enough to worry about with the Awakening and all that stuff. I felt kind of selfish now, and was glad I had joined the cause.

"Now we're going to be entering Inferno. It's a town run by demons that's unstable, but we're close to taking it back. They don't have walls up or guarded checkpoints, so we're able to infiltrate it more easily. Some of the more outlying towns, deeper into their hold, are much more secure," Lincoln explained, as our bus crawled deeper into the smoky black night.

I raised my hand and Lincoln nodded in my direction.

"Inferno?" I asked.

Lincoln smirked. "We've named all of the local demon strongholds after the levels of Hell in Dante's *Inferno*. The city of Treacherous, formerly San Francisco, is the most powerful demon stronghold in the world."

I wanted to chuckle at the silly names, but his statement gave me chills. It reminded me that we were a small part of a very big problem that extended all over the world. Every major city, in every state, in every country was divided—Angel City on one side and Demon City on the other.

When the bus dipped onto a side road, I saw streetlights up ahead, and the buildings looked more and more put together. Lincoln's hand moved to rest on the butt of his gun as we rolled closer to Inferno.

"I want everyone to just look outside the windows, and get accustomed to this town, because it's our current base. The goal is to take it back, then extend the wall of Angel City out here, and start cleaning it up," Lincoln announced. "But that's obviously confidential. Fallen family only," he added.

"Fallen family" was another word for the army. That meant any of this intel could be shared among others in the Fallen Army but no civilians.

Wow, we're going to be taking an entire city back from the demons? The thought was both thrilling and terrifying.

As we pulled onto the main road, I started to hear music and saw a hustle and bustle of people scurrying along the sidewalks.

My eyes landed on a Mugwort demon. They were total alcoholics, and you could tell one not just by the yellowish bone-colored horns that protruded off their warty faces, but also by their drunken walk. The one I saw now was swaying with a beer in his hand, singing something.

Shea and I kicked one in the balls once. They were lecherous assholes, constantly hitting on women. The one Shea and I had attacked had been too hammered to retaliate, so luckily, we'd gotten away scot-free.

As if he wanted to prove my thought, I saw the Mugwort demon reach out to a passing woman who looked human and grab her ass.

I waited for her to smack him with her purse, or flip him off, or at least scowl, but she didn't. She just gave him a hollow look and kept walking, like maybe she'd been grabbed too many times to react anymore.

Oh God.

It was such a small thing to notice, but it affected me deeply, as deeply as if I'd seen an innocent woman murdered or raped. Because they were the same. They'd broken that woman's spirit, and that was as horrifying as death to me.

My eyes flew to a street fight that was in progress, and I gasped when I saw it was children. The two boys didn't look more than twelve years old, but they were throwing punches that resembled those of a trained fighter. Demons stood in a circle around them, cheering them on, and waving dollar bills in the air.

No.

"Don't look away." Lincoln's voice shook me from my trance, and I pulled my eyes from the fight to see him speaking to one of the other rookies on our team—Valerie, a Necromancer. "You have to see what we're up against, and you have to get the shock over with, because the next time we bring you in here, we're going to need your help. We need to save these people, and we can't do it without you," he declared.

Something unfurled in my chest then. A deep purpose was growing within me; I was having a total paradigm shift. I no longer wanted to just get by and have a job for money. I wanted to fight, I wanted to be the greatest soldier the Fallen Army had ever seen, and I wanted to kill every demon on this earth. I also wanted to be a healer like Noah, running out into the trenches, and healing humans from their demon-inflicted injuries. The two opposites warred inside of me.

Lincoln's eyes met mine and something passed between us. I could see it in his eyes—this was his passion too. Each time he came out here, I wondered why he kept coming back. He was always getting injured, or was gone for weeks at a time, but now I knew. We needed to liberate these people.

I needed to find James. My old friend from Demon City was Sighted. He would be able to tell me if the prophecy regarding Lucifer and me was true. Because if it was, I was going to kill that bastard. Even if it cost me my life. I wanted the world back the way it was when I was a kid. Yeah, bad shit still happened, but nothing like this. If I could do that, then I could think of nothing better for which to live my life.

Lincoln's walkie-talkie squawked, interrupting my life-pondering.

"All available units near Madison and 4th, requesting help. I've got a Succubus demon trying to take a little girl. Repeat, all available units, please respond." Lincoln's eyes widened and we all just stared at him. He wasn't answering the call.

What the hell is a Succubus demon? I'd never seen or heard of one, other than in horror films.

"Someone else will answer. We're not taking calls

tonight," Lincoln told the van filled with terrified rookies.

Standing, Noah walked to the front of the bus, where Lincoln's hand was poised over the walkie-talkie.

"Mayday!" The voice came back, more urgent that time. "All available units to Madison and 4th. This innocent kid is going to die!" he shouted.

Lincoln cursed and picked up the walkie-talkie as Noah instructed our driver.

"Lieutenant Lincoln Grey here. I'm with a team of rooks on a sightseeing quest, not cleared for missions. What's your status?"

"Lincoln! It's Tanner," a new voice came over the walkie. "We're at the Madison Apartments doing our street patrol, and the girl's mom ran out screaming for us. I tried to enter the apartment, but the Succubus threw me across the room. She's already taken one kid. They were twins."

My whole body flinched as bile rose in my throat. "Tell him we're coming!" I shouted and stood.

Were. He said they were twins. That meant...

Lincoln cut me a glare and spoke into the walkie. "Noah and I are coming to assist. I'll have the driver take my rooks back to Angel City. ETA two minutes."

Pushing out of my seat, I beelined it for my boyfriend. My drill sergeant. My asshole, who was about to tell me I couldn't go inside.

79

I tried to lower my voice. "*Sir*, we may not be trained for missions, but we all passed the gauntlet. If it means saving this little kid's life, then let us help you."

Lincoln looked down at me like I was a child. "Do you know what a Succubus demon is? Have you ever seen one?"

I squirmed, holding onto the rail as we took a hard turn. "No."

Lincoln looked pleased with himself, as if he'd won some battle with me. "It's the only female demon we've ever seen, and she's a fucking *nightmare*. She feeds off children's fear and bad dreams, which usually kills them from the shock. Then she escapes into open portals back to Hell, which she leaves open so more demons can filter through."

I winced.

"Oh, and she shoots razor blades from her mouth for fun," Lincoln added.

Well, that definitely didn't sound awesome, but it only served to reinforce my point. "You can't take her on with only four of you. You need all of us, especially me. I have dark magic, and I can use it against her."

It was the first time in a long time that I'd ever thought about using it.

"We're going!" Shea shouted and stood. I turned around to see the other rookies suiting up, adjusting their weapons and tightening belts.

Lincoln gave me a death glare. "Has anyone ever told you that you're really bad at obeying orders?"

I nodded. "All the time. So what's the plan?"

Lincoln sighed, his eyes dropping to my wrist cuffs.

"You have Sera?" he asked.

I pulled her from my thigh holster.

Lincoln looked back at Noah, who nodded.

"Okay, here's the plan. Noah, the other two senior Fallen Army guards, and I will go in first. We alone will battle the Succubus while you guys split into three groups. The first group will grab the dead child's body and bring it back to the van so this poor mother can have a proper burial. The second group will grab the other little girl, hopefully still alive, and ferry her to the van to be with her mother."

We all nodded our understanding, and then he looked at Shea. "You closed that Hell portal one time. Think you can do it again?"

Shea nodded without hesitation. "Absolutely." She'd been working with Mr. Claymore in her advanced independent study, and was doing all kinds of stuff she shouldn't know how to do yet.

"The third group, which will consist of Luke, Shea, and Brielle, will close the portal and make sure everyone gets out of the apartment alive," he finished with a heavy sigh.

I nodded. He was letting me go in, giving me a big job, and I wasn't even nervous. That was weird.

Noah crossed the space, and placed a hand on my shoulder. "You're the only healer here besides Lincoln and me. Remember that. If the girl is injured and it's minor, you can help heal her while we're battling the Succubus."

I gave him a curt nod. I forgot sometimes that I was all of those things: fighter, healer, part angel, part dark magic wielder.

Lincoln threw a sideways glance at me. "Don't be a hero. Let us handle this, and you just extract the little girl. Do you understand, Atwater?"

Me? Be the hero? Never.

I grinned. "Yes, sir."

Our bus pulled up to the curb, where I could see two Fallen Army soldiers comforting a grieving mother.

Lincoln held the walkie to his mouth. "All available units make your way to Madison Apartments. We're going in to sequester the Succubus."

The radio squawked. "I'm inbound, but I'm a good twenty minutes from you," said a familiar voice over the radio. Darren.

"She'll be dead by then," Lincoln told us. Over the radio, he simply acknowledged Darren, and then we were moving out.

"Luke, can you shift for me? I might need you to knock the door in," Lincoln asked the Beast Shifter.

Luke nodded. "Men, always using me just for my body," he joked and then disappeared behind some bushes. The two Fallen Army soldiers helped the grieving mother onto the bus, then gave Lincoln and the group a rundown of the situation.

"She's powerful. She chucked me across the room like a tornado," one soldier said. I glanced down at the insignia on his chest to see he was a Necromancer.

Lincoln nodded. "Let's move. We don't have a lot of time."

We quickly split up into three groups, while the driver stayed behind to keep the mother on the bus.

As we were taking the steps up to the second floor, Luke roared behind us, announcing his presence.

"You scared the shit out of me!" Shea shrieked at him as his fur brushed against my leg. He bounded along beside us and then squeezed past me, knocking my body into Shea. Soon he was at the front of the line, right beside Lincoln.

It was in that moment that I heard the small, yet mighty, scream of a child. Adrenaline pulsed through me, and emotion tightened my throat. I wasn't sure there was anything else in the world that motivated a soldier more than the wail of a helpless child.

Lincoln jiggled the door handle and then nodded to Luke.

"We're on borrowed time!" Lincoln shouted, pulling his sword as blue splinters of light shot from the blade.

Luke wasted no time, rearing up on his hind legs, and then charging the door. Putting all of his probably five-hundred-pound weight into the push, he came down on top of it. The door was one of those cheaper aluminum ones, so instead of cracking or falling apart, it simply burst off the hinges and then fell flat onto the floor, revealing an apartment.

Lincoln waited for no one, charging past Luke and running headfirst into the house. My man was fearless. I hadn't yet decided if that was a good or a bad thing.

We all waited as Lincoln, Noah, and the other two Fallen Army soldiers ran into the apartment. Then the first team went in—the one tasked with removing the dead little girl's body. My heart ached at the very thought of seeing a dead child. I had every intention of being a good girl and awaiting Lincoln's next instructions until I heard Bonnie's call for help.

"She's not dead!" my classmate screamed.

Instinct took over then. Bonnie was a Necromancer—she knew death. If she said the little girl wasn't dead, she wasn't dead. I was the only healer available, so if the little girl needed help, it was going to have to come from me.

The second I started for the door, Shea and Luke trailed behind me without question.

"What are you doing?" the second group whispered. They were waiting by the door for Lincoln's okay to come get the second twin.

"Don't worry," I told them, and then I was in the apartment.

As I entered the space, the first thing that hit me was the smell. It was surprisingly sweet and alluring—vanilla, but with an underlying decaying odor.

There were some gnarly battle sounds coming from the bedroom, and it took everything in me not to go in there, and try to help out. I had to trust that Lincoln had this handled.

'If he doesn't, I'm ready,' Sera told me. I patted her hilt in an effort to calm her. I had every intention of *not* seeing that Succubus.

"In here!" Bonnie whisper-screamed, and I turned toward the sound. They were all hunched over a small child's form, and the familiar swirls of purple and orange Necromancer magic—that I'd grown up seeing with my mom—were dancing around the little girl's body.

I frowned. "I thought you said she wasn't dead?" The little girl's brunette hair was cropped short and splayed out onto the carpet behind her, and she was seemingly lifeless. If she wasn't dead, why was Bonnie using Necro magic? Even if she was, why the hell was Bonnie using Necro magic? Besides it being forbidden to raise the dead in Angel City, it was doubly forbidden to raise a child.

Bonnie held her hands over the girl. "She's kind of half in, half out. Her soul keeps jumping from that room back here into her body. I'm trying to pin it into her," Bonnie explained.

85

That was some crazy shit. My mom tried to explain to me once how she knew someone was dead even from twenty feet away. It was the light, the aura, the soul. Necromancers could see it, sense it, and manipulate it at times. It kind of freaked me out.

"Can you force it down? Then, maybe I could heal her." Bending down, I ran my hands over the little girl, trying to do a healing scan. It was a third-year study but Noah had shown me a little so I was going to wing it. She was human, obviously, and therefore quite frail from the trauma. There would be no supernatural healing kicking in for her.

Bonnie shook her head. "This is some advanced shit. The Succubus in the room is doing something. I'm pulling against her."

I breathed in and out slowly, trying to feel for something I could heal, but there was nothing I could sense that needed healing. Her life-force felt so weak, and I wasn't sure how to help that. I needed to work on my healing skills with Noah more.

"Lincoln, look out!" I heard one of the boys call from the room, and then a crashing sound rang throughout the house.

Screw the rules.

I pulled Sera from my thigh holster and took off running to the bedroom. I wasn't going to let some little demon bitch hurt my man and steal this little girl's soul.

I have the mark of Lucifer himself, and I'm not scared of any demon. They should be scared of me!

With all the confidence of a lioness, I ripped the door open and readied myself for a fight. But when my gaze fell onto the creature suspended in midair, I nearly pissed myself.

"Holy shitballs." I breathed.

And then she tried to kill me.

CHAPTER 8

I GREW UP AROUND DEMONS. WARTS, OOZING SKIN, horns, scales—none of it scared me. But the creature before me now was absolutely terrifying.

She was humanoid-looking with long, thin silvery hair, and gaunt cheeks that made her look even more ghoulish. Her body was waif-thin, showing protruding bones from every angle. That was okay—a skinny demon, I could handle—but her eyes were…missing. Where a human would have eyes, she had black empty pits, and yet she looked right at me. Her hands were weapons themselves. The fingers didn't seem to have skin; they were just sharpened bones that turned into claws, and glowed an angry red. She was grinning in my direction, and I saw a legit razor blade peeking out from behind her teeth.

I guess Lincoln wasn't joking about that part.
Lord have mercy.

Everything happened so quickly that I could barely process it. I did a rapid scan of the room to see both of the Fallen Army guards unconscious on the floor and Noah leaning over one of them, healing orange light emanating from his palms. Lincoln was crouched over a terrified, pale, stricken little girl identical to the one in the living room. His sword and gun were drawn and he looked feral. Blood dripped from his left eyebrow and down his cheek.

The Succubus was already halfway to me, crawling across the ceiling like a possessed monkey. My name burst from Lincoln's lips, but all I could hear was my heartbeat slamming in my ears. My eyes flicked once again to the little girl and how terrified she looked. This evil demon was feeding off them and had nearly killed her sister in the other room.

Anger boiled inside of me and I just…reacted. Sera told me nothing, and gave me no advice; I just exploded. I leaped into the air to meet the demon instead of falling back. With a roar, I lashed out, and Sera shot a bolt of white-hot light from her blade that licked across the demon's abdomen, cutting it open.

Holy shit.

I barely had time to register how badass Sera was, and that she'd cut the demon without touching her, when a razor blade flew across the room and sank into my left upper arm. Pain shot up my muscles, as I fell backward with all the grace of a giant elephant. The Succubus didn't let up—she was coming for me full throttle.

"Brielle!" Lincoln roared, but didn't leave the little girl's side.

Rage boiled hotter inside of me and I did a kick-up, throwing my legs into the air and forward, allowing the motion to pull my body into a standing position. A little something Darren taught me. The demon dropped from the ceiling like a freaking hundred-pound spider, landing right on top of me. Her hip hit my head, throwing me to the side, and then I felt her searing-hot claws on my back. I'd fallen to my knees with her weight, but her leg was right in front of me, and I took the opportunity to shove Sera in, right up to the hilt.

A roar rang out from the demon and she pulled herself off me, standing before me with those two red glowing hands outstretched.

"Lucifer's princess," she cooed in a voice that was anything but human. Her gaping eye sockets were locked on my chest and the mark that rested there.

She put one hand on Sera's hilt, pulling her out without a problem.

Shit.

'She's made of fire. I can't burn her,' Sera told me.

I lunged for my weapon just as the Succubus thrust her arm out and an invisible force knocked into me, throwing me backward out of the room and into the entryway.

Shea and Luke scream-roared simultaneously. I landed hard on my ass, but immediately righted myself. The Succubus had gone back into the room, and was doing some weird shit with her hands, Sera still clutched in her grip.

'Get me out of here!' Sera screamed, panicked.

The darkness inside of me was welling up. I couldn't push it down any longer, nor did I want to do it.

The Succubus had her back to me as she opened a portal on the wall. Lincoln had the little girl draped in his arms, and was standing at the far end of the room. He was inching along the wall, trying to make it to me, and the open doorway.

Does that demon bitch think she's going to leave with my freaking seraph blade?!

Noah was still helping the two soldiers. When my eyes flicked to Lincoln, he shook his head. A big fat no from him.

Screw that. Sera was a part of me; I wasn't just letting her go.

I screamed and thrust my arms out, intending for the black blob to rise out of my throat, like it normally did, and wrap around her neck. That didn't happen. Instead, a shiny, black energy whip burst from my palm and coiled around the demon's waist.

Holy mother of darkness.

The demon hissed, and then everything happened seemingly in slow motion. She swung her arm, and I watched Sera swirl through the air and into the Hell portal.

'Bri!' Sera shouted, and I felt a physical pain in my chest as she sailed through the opening and was lost into oblivion. All I could see was red haze and fire.

The Succubus spun on me then. I was without my cherished weapon, but I had a new one. A totally freaky and really dark weapon, but it was a weapon nonetheless. I cinched the whip tighter and she roared.

"Whatever you're doing is working!" Bonnie yelled from the next room.

The little girl. I could save her. I may have lost Sera, but I could save the girl.

With all my strength, I wrapped both hands around the whip and yanked.

"Nooooo," the Succubus yelled, pushing her hands outward. That invisible force knocked into me again, but when I went flying, I made sure to hold the black energy whip tight. It pulled her with me, and I saw rivulets of dark inky blood fall from her stomach as the whip cut into her. She was clawing at it frantically, and just behind her, I spotted Lincoln approaching with his blazing sword in his hands. I quickly flicked my eyes down to the ground so she wouldn't notice my attention on him.

She must have sensed him though, because as he came down on her neck, she turned, but it was too late. Her head flew from her body and hit the wall with a thud.

My whip disintegrated and I was flung backward with the sudden loss of tension, but I was able to roll my body to the side so my fall wasn't severe. I immediately jumped up, searching for the portal. My eyes flicked to the wall where it once stood, and my stomach dropped as I noticed it had snapped closed with the Succubus's death.

"Sera," I whimpered as tears filled my eyes.

Lincoln frowned, looking lost. "We'll figure it out. What's going on with the other girl?"

Right. I needed to keep it together for the little girl.

"Noah! We need help. She's still alive," I informed the healer.

I glanced around the room. The one little girl Lincoln had been protecting was sitting on the bed crying. He had tied a cloth around her eyes so she couldn't see what happened, while Noah helped the two other soldiers, who were now conscious and sitting up. He stood and nodded for me to lead the way.

Again, I looked back at where the portal had been.

"You can't," Lincoln said sternly.

I wanted to have Shea open it back up and go in after her, even though I knew it was insane.

'Sera? Can you hear me?' I asked as I led Noah

into the living room, and pointed to where the little girl was lying. She was moving now and moaning, thank God.

No response from Sera.

As Noah went to work on the girl with Bonnie's assistance, I turned to Lincoln.

"Are you okay?" he asked, pulling my hands into his and turning the palms up to the ceiling as he checked them out.

The black magic whip. I'd almost forgotten.

"Sera" was all I said. It felt like I'd just watched a cherished friend or family member fall into that pit.

Lincoln frowned. "Yeah... We'll figure that out. I'll ask Raph."

He was stroking my wrists, but I pulled them back and met his eyes. "I don't want to talk about that." I indicated my hands.

"It was pretty incredible," Lincoln hedged.

My emotions were raw from the loss of Sera, and now I had yet another dark gift. I couldn't deal with it.

"Lincoln," I warned.

He nodded. "Let's get the girls in the van and head back to Angel City."

I frowned. "We're not leaving them?"

Lincoln's face hardened. "No way. More Succubi might come back. I'll sneak them in if I have to."

I nodded, taking a look over his shoulder. "Maybe if I could just have Shea open it, for one minute..."

Lincoln looked at me agonizingly. "Something else could crawl through. We need to get these girls to their mother."

I swallowed my selfishness and nodded. Now wasn't the right time, but I would get her back. That was for sure.

———•·—

I didn't have kids yet, obviously, but I knew what it was like to lose someone. The day my father died changed me forever. It had completely ripped me open, and in trying to put myself back together, the pieces never fit right.

When the mother on the bus saw both of her daughters were indeed alive, she fell apart, and we all fell apart right along with her. The relief and joy she felt was tangible. Even Lincoln looked a bit misty-eyed, but he quickly brushed it off, and ordered us in the bus.

As we were making our way out of Inferno, Lincoln got on his cell phone and called Archangel Michael.

He had his cell number.

No big deal.

"Hello, sir. Can you talk for a minute?" Lincoln asked.

I leaned forward in my seat so when he lowered his voice, I could still eavesdrop.

"I've got three civilians, a mother and two little girls. We just saved them from a Succubus demon, and I need to get them into Angel City tonight," Lincoln explained.

Something Michael said must have pissed him off, because his face turned menacing. "I don't care if the shelters are full."

More listening. More anger. "She's a free soul. What about a transfer to San Diego?"

Free soul. That term still made me angry inside. I hadn't even noticed her forehead was free of the demon mark. Lincoln was always looking for things like that.

My poor mother. Will he ever trust her?

"What if I can find them housing?" Lincoln asked.

There was a pause. He was scowling.

"Yes, sir. I know." Lincoln sounded dejected. A shadow crossed his face, and then his scowl morphed into a look of determination. "I've secured them housing, sir."

I frowned. *Huh?*

That fast, without making a call? Michael must have been as confused as I was.

"Yes, sir, you have my word. Long-term housing for all three of them." Now Lincoln was smiling, looking pleased with himself.

He finally ended the call, and I met his gaze. "What housing did you secure?" I whispered.

He raised one eyebrow. "You were listening?"

I rolled my eyes. "Linc, where are they gonna go?"

Running a hand through his hair, he sighed. "I had a two-bedroom apartment through the army when my parents died. Part of my compensation package. I'll ask to be reassigned a place, and they can stay in my trailer."

My heart burst into tiny emoji hearts that floated around his head. Or at least it felt like that's what it would do if this were a cartoon. "Where will you sleep in the meantime?"

"I'll crash on Noah's couch." His dark lashes framed his crystalline blue eyes, making them pop and look arresting.

"You're amazing," I told him. "Seriously."

He gave me a weak smile. "We saved three tonight, but there are millions more, and with the shelters full and Angel City against seeing homeless tent cities…it's not enough. But I helped a little."

I could see now that he tortured himself over this. Lincoln Grey would not rest until every free soul was saved.

I didn't want to be the one to break it to him, but that just wasn't possible.

CHAPTER 9

THE NEXT THREE WEEKS WERE HARD EMOTION-
ally. Sera was gone, and Mikey still hadn't
shifted back to human. He was missing school, and
my mom and I were going stir-crazy not being able
to see him. I had a phone meeting with Clark, his
alpha, after my history class, which I was barely
paying attention to, focusing more on making the
call.

"The underworld, Hell, down there. Whatever
you call it, today we are going to learn all about it,"
Mrs. Delacourt trilled.

My attention was pulled to the front. I still
wasn't used to seeing Centaurs. Mrs. Delacourt was
a magnificent white horse on her lower half and a
tanned Greek goddess on her upper.

"The realm where the Prince of Darkness rules, lies directly under our world," she called out.

More than a few eyes landed on me when she mentioned Lucifer. I'd taken to wearing high-collared shirts to hide my mark, but it was useless since everyone already knew it was there. I'd come to terms with the fact that the mark would be a part of me forever.

"If I were to open a portal today and look through, then open a portal next week and look through, I could see the same swatch of landscape. That tells us that the underworld doesn't move or shift."

Interesting. I immediately thought of Sera.

A hand shot up, and I inwardly groaned to see it was Tiffany.

"Yes, Tiffany." Was that a curled upper lip I detected from the professor?

The blonde Light Mage wiggled in her seat. "Is it true that Celestials can't go there? That it's, like, a thousand times worse for them there than it would be in Demon City?"

I glared at Tiffany. What an annoying and stupid question.

"Yes, that's true. They've tried, and crossing the threshold inflicts so much pain that it brings the person near death," the professor admitted.

Tiffany glanced back at me. "But for someone who has no problem in Demon City, someone demon gifted, they'd be fine in Hell, right?"

Bitch. Why was murder illegal? Some people just shouldn't be allowed to live.

Mrs. Delacourt glared at Tiffany. "Hypothetically, yes. Moving on."

As our history professor started to draw a diagram on the board, I stared at the back of Tiffany's glossy blonde hair and thought of all the ways I could inflict harm on her.

———•·—•———

"I just want to see him. Just for a minute, to make sure he's okay," I pleaded with Clark.

"No." Clark's firm commanding voice flared through the phone, getting on my last nerve.

"He's my brother!" I shouted.

"Yes he is. And how would he feel if he mauled you to death?" he snapped back.

Geeze.

This guy really had a way with people.

"My mom's really worried and losing sleep over this. Can't you tell us anything?" I decided playing the sappy mom card might work.

Clark sighed, followed by a long stretch of silence before he spoke. "Mikey is showing signs of being a lone wolf. He's rejecting the pack and my lead. But at the same time, he needs us or he'll be lost to the beast. If he doesn't turn back to human before the next full moon, he may be too far gone for me to bring him back."

My whole entire body sagged as I slid against the wall in my dorm room, emotion tightening my throat.

"Oh my God."

Mikey was my little brother. I felt completely responsible for him.

Clark sighed again. "Look, kid, was there some trauma when you were younger or something? It's like he wants to stay like this. He's avoiding his humanity for a reason, which happens in cases where they went through some tough shit they didn't properly deal with. The beast brings it all out and forces them to deal with it to make them stronger."

Trauma.

That word was ugly. It meant you'd endured something horrific that left a lasting impression. But it was also accurate.

"My mom and I sold ourselves to the demons to heal my dad's cancer when I was twelve. He was hit by a bus six months later and died."

"Oh God." Clark's voice, for the first time, was full of empathy. "Yeah, that'll do it."

My whole world felt like it was caving in around me.

"Can you... I dunno, try harder? Get a shrink out there? Something." I had reached the point of begging. If my dad's death and my mom's and my demon enslavement were messing with Mikey, I felt totally responsible.

101

"I'm doing the best I can, but I can try something different. Was your dad buried anywhere? You have ashes or anything?"

His question caught me off guard. When my dad died, we all agreed as a family that we didn't want him buried in Demon City. It was nearly a month's salary, but my mom bought him a plot in Angel City at the prettiest Catholic cemetery. We'd all gotten day passes, and she was given the time off work to lay him to rest. I'd been so used to not being able to see him that I didn't even think of visiting him now that I lived here. Until now.

"Immaculate Heart in Culver City. Daniel Atwater is his name." Speaking his name after so long sent tears leaking from the corner of my eyes. Thank God I was alone in my room, because this call had been way more intense than I'd intended. Some serious ugly crying was about to happen.

"All right, kid. I'll keep you posted. Give me a week."

A week? Then what? I didn't want to know.

"Okay," I croaked.

He hung up, and I shoved my face into the pillow and screamed. I screamed with pain, rage, and utter desperation. I felt like I was so full of all of those emotions that they would drown me if I didn't let them out. Too much was going wrong lately. I'd lost Sera, my devil mark was permanent, my brother was stuck as a beast, and I wasn't totally convinced I was going to get my mom out of Demon City.

I needed something, just one thing, to go right.

My phone buzzed with a text.

Mr. Rincor: Are you coming to class?

Shit! I was his only student, so it was kind of hard to ditch. With Fred graduated, and my twenty-watt bulb hands, I'd tried to drop the class, but Mr. Rincor wouldn't let me.

Jumping off the bed, I wiped my eyes, and put all thoughts of my brother out of my mind as I grabbed my bag.

I texted Mr. Rincor that I had a family emergency and would be there in five minutes, then hauled ass out of my dorm and into the open quad.

Lincoln was just leaving Raphael's office. When he saw me, a smile lit up his face and he called me over.

"Hey, what are you doing here?" I asked him. "I thought you had work." He was supposed to be out there doing army stuff today.

He held up a pair of keys. "Raphael called me in early. I got my new apartment assignment. A two-bedroom three doors down from Noah."

I raised my eyebrows in appraisal. "Not too shabby, Mr. Grey."

He grinned. "And Raphael gave the groundskeeper

job to Mrs. Finley, so she and her girls can get out of my cramped trailer and have the cottage."

"Wow, that's awesome!" Of course, that made me think of Mikey, since he'd lived in the cottage for a short time, but when he got back, he'd be in the dorms with me, and that was good. I didn't want to bring up Mikey now and ruin the moment of happiness about his new place.

He looked off into the open space. "Guess I don't need my trailer anymore. Maybe it's time to sell it."

I frowned at the idea. After all, he'd told me it was his parents' camping trailer and full of happy memories. Selling it would be a mistake. "No way. It's a badass little pad. Just hang on to it for a while. No need to make rash decisions."

He nodded, grinning, and pulling me in for a kiss. "Small gathering at my new place tonight. Bring your friends."

My lips curled into a smile, and I'd stepped up on my tiptoes to kiss him again when a loud throat clearing sounded behind me.

I craned my neck to see Mr. Rincor and Mr. Claymore standing there. Whoops.

Lincoln took a step back. "See you later," he said and bailed.

I winced, turning to fully face my professors. "Sorry. I really did have a family thing. My brother..." I let the sentence hang in the air as a thought struck me.

Why is Mr. Claymore here?

Mr. Rincor nodded. "I'm aware of the sensitive situation. Mr. Claymore has made you something. Please join us in the classroom." His voice was monotone, but his words spoke volumes.

What the hell would the head Light Mage have for me? Was I in trouble?

The two tall men simply led the way inside as I shuffled behind them, a jumble of nerves.

Once we entered the small classroom, I set my bag down and stared at my palms. This class was so defeating. Every time Mr. Rincor tried to work with me, it either yielded super unimpressive twenty-watt lightbulb results, or some dark blob flew from my palms.

Mr. Claymore pulled up a chair and set an amulet on the table. It was a mixture of silver and gold, in a braided chain with a large two-inch clear pearlescent oval stone pendant.

My eyes widened. "Whoa, is that for me?"

He chuckled. "Normally it would be inappropriate for a teacher to give a student jewelry, but yes, it's for you."

I raised one eyebrow. "What is it?"

Clearly this wasn't a normal pendant.

His lips quirked. "Brielle, you're a Celestial blessed by four angels. There is no way you do not carry their light inside of you."

His words shook me. After the Lucifer tattoo, the

dark magic and all that, I hadn't realized how much I needed to hear that. My eyes grew misty.

"But my light…it's broken." I gestured to my hands. When that Succubus had tried to attack me, light hadn't shot out of my hands, darkness had.

He shook his head and picked up the necklace. "I think it's hiding. I can't remove the Dark Prince's mark, but I can trap the dark powers within you."

With that statement, he confirmed it. I had dark powers. I hadn't even told him yet about the black whip I could produce. But his words about containing it gave me hope.

"So I wear this and no more dark blobs flying out?" I reached for the pendant.

He nodded. "That's right. Unless you take it off."

My heart pained then, Sera wasn't here to experience this with me. She'd be so happy for me. I missed her. It'd been too long, but I couldn't come up with a viable plan about how to get her back. Shea said she'd open a portal for me and I could try to call to her, but that was a huge risk and a shot in the dark. Especially after learning from my history class that our world directly overlaid Hell. Sera would be back in Inferno, unless someone in Hell moved her. That was a possibility I couldn't even think about.

Mr. Claymore stood and took the necklace, attaching it around my neck. The moment the stone rested against the tattooed mark on my chest, I felt a tingle throughout my body as a weight seemingly lifted from me.

"Whoa," I whispered. Taking in a deep breath, I felt lighter than ever before, as if the stress I'd been carrying, the self-doubt and worry just…disappeared.

"Feel something? That's a good sign," Mr. Claymore added.

Footsteps approached as Mr. Rincor made his way over to my desk.

"All right, Brielle. I have a feeling this has been our roadblock. Let's give it a go now, what do you say?"

My light studies professor was so patient and sweet with me. We'd been through a lot on my journey, including months of him telling me just to not use my powers, and nearly giving up on me. There was a time when we'd both admitted I may not have light powers within me beyond my barely glowing palms. But now… Now I had hope, which was a good and dangerous thing. Hope could let you down, but it could also redeem you.

I nodded nervously as the two professors stepped behind me. They weren't worried about getting blasted with light. No, they stepped behind me because when I usually tried this, dark magic flew out of me and tried to hurt whoever was in my way.

Holding my hands up, I pointed them in front of me at the vacant room.

"I'm nervous." The confession flew from my lips.

"Whatever happens, or doesn't happen, it's okay, Brielle," Mr. Rincor's smooth voice assured from behind me.

Okay. Here goes nothing.

I wish Sera was here.

Taking a deep breath, I felt for my Celestial power, which was a bit like a buzzing electrical feeling. It was always there but only awakened when I focused on it. Shining my attention on it now, I felt the high-wire buzz run throughout my body, stronger than ever before.

Maybe this *was* going to work.

One more deep breath and I pushed, hard. A bright buttery yellow light shot from my hands and illuminated the room, forcing me to turn my head, and stumble backward to avoid blindness.

"Holy mother of Mary," Mr. Rincor breathed.

I shook my hands, trying to dim my power, but there was still an immense glow. Turning to look at my palms, I saw the glow was no longer there, but in the middle of the room was a floating, glowing...orb.

"What the heck is that?" I asked.

Mr. Rincor stepped out from behind me, his jaw slack and his eyes wide. "*That* is an archangel power. A Celestial orb."

I swallowed hard. "Okay, but what exactly does it do?"

Mr. Rincor walked over to the far wall where a

few swords were mounted and pulled one off. Then he approached the orb and dipped the sword into it.

"Be careful," I deadpanned.

Now Mr. Claymore had walked out and was staring curiously at the spectacle before us. He seemed as baffled as I was.

Mr. Rincor pulled the sword from the orb and it was...on fire. Well, that wasn't quite right. It was glowing with...light.

"Watch this," the light studies professor warned. Then he brought the sword down slowly into one of the desks and cut through it like butter. It crashed in half, falling to the floor, and leaving Mr. Claymore and me with our eyebrows raised.

"Um, is that normal? That I made that?" I hated that word, *normal*, but I also desperately yearned to be normal. Catch-22.

Mr. Rincor looked at me with blazing blue eyes. "It's incredible. This could change the war. If you were to make these orbs and leave them for the troops in the war zones, it would greatly improve our odds."

I swallowed hard.

"Let's talk to Raphael. She's still learning." Mr. Claymore laid a protective hand on my shoulder.

"Of course," Mr. Rincor stated, looking a bit guilty. "In time, I meant."

We all stared at the glowing orb.

"So, what do we do with it?" Mr. Claymore finally asked.

Mr. Rincor rubbed his chin. "You can throw an Abrus demon into one of these things, and they'll dissolve. But it could also hurt a student, so I'll have to have Raphael break it down."

Right. Okay. Basically I was a dangerous weapon. *Awesome.*

The professor turned to me. "Let's hold off on doing that again until class on Monday. We'll go for something less grand." He winked.

I nodded, chuckling. "You got it."

To be honest, it had taken a lot out of me; I was ready to take a nap after that energy outburst.

Mr. Claymore motioned to the necklace. "Keep it on and I think you won't have any…unpleasant magical issues anymore." He meant the dark magic, of course. The unpleasant "magical issue" was that I had Lucifer's archangel power inside of me, to a certain degree.

I just nodded, feeling drained of energy all of a sudden.

"Can we end class early? I'm tired," I confessed to the two gentlemen.

Mr. Rincor shook himself. "Oh, of course. You'll probably be drained for a few days. That much light leaving you all at once is…something."

I just bobbed my head and shuffled out of the room. Since this was my last class, I decided to go back to the dorm and take a nap.

Pulling out my phone, I shot Shea a quick text

telling her about Lincoln's party tonight, and asked her to wake me if I wasn't up by dinner.

I felt like I'd been hit by a truck. The moment I saw my bed, I crashed onto it, and all thought left me as the fatigue won over.

CHAPTER 10

I T TOOK SHEA LIKE TEN TRIES TO WAKE ME, AND I'D ended up chugging an iced coffee just to get some of my energy back. Now, we were parking at Lincoln's new apartment complex, slightly off campus, in the Fallen Army housing compound called Lighthouse Villas.

"So... Noah asked me to sleep over at his house tonight. I told him I'd think about it," Shea told me as I put the car in park.

The time had come to have the real 'tough love' talk with this woman. I turned to my best friend. "Do you love him?" I asked bluntly.

She swallowed hard and then nodded.

"Do you trust him?"

She chewed her lip. "You know that's hard for me."

Yeah, it was. Growing up with a vacant deadbeat dad, and her mom leaving her for drugs had messed her up. It was hard, but she needed to learn something…

"Not everyone is like your dad or mom, Shea."

Tears welled in her eyes and she nodded. "I know that."

Reaching out, I grasped her hand. "I think you and Noah have reached the jumping-off point. Either dive in or walk away, because it's not fair to him to keep stringing him along, if you're not capable of emotionally investing in him fully."

Shea laughed. "Wow, when did you become a shrink?"

I chuckled. "I'm just saying it's okay to put yourself out there, to trust. I don't think Noah would ever intentionally hurt you."

She nodded. "I totally started messing around with him at first for fun. But now…"

"Now it's love," I finished for her, with a squeeze of her hand.

She sighed. "Yeah."

"Which is a good thing! The world needs more love," I declared.

Shea grinned and reached in the back seat of my Fallen Academy-issued SUV, producing a large backpack. "Okay good, because I totally packed an overnight bag."

Laughter bubbled out of me. "You crack me up."

She peeked in her bag. "I brought five condoms. Do you think that will be enough?"

"Oh my God, Shea!" I gasped and then laughed again. "If that's not enough, then you guys need to enter the sex Olympics."

Shea just rolled her eyes, but then her face grew serious. "Is that a thing?"

Oh my God.

Shaking my head, I opened the door. "Come on. We're late."

I was going to need an energy drink if this fatigue kept up. I was seriously exhausted. The sheer act of walking was tiring, so when I saw there was no elevator, and remembered Lincoln was on the third floor, I groaned.

My legs were heavy sacks of Jell-O by the time we made it up there. Before we even got to the door, it flew open.

"A Celestial orb!" Lincoln shouted at me.

I guess privacy isn't something I'm going to be allowed in this lifetime. "Who told you?" I demanded.

He raised one eyebrow as Shea slipped past him and went inside.

"Why didn't *you* tell me is the bigger question here." His words were laced with hurt.

I rolled my eyes. "I was going to once we walked inside. You beat me to it. I've been passed out for the past three hours trying to regain my energy."

His tough guy routine immediately fell. "What do you mean? Are you hurt?"

"Nah, just tired as all hell." I waved him off. "That... thing zapped all my energy."

Lincoln reached out and stroked the pendant at my neck.

"So... Who told you?" I asked again.

Lincoln sighed. "Raphael said he needed to go break down a Celestial orb on campus. Since Michael, Gabriel, and Uriel were out of town, I asked him who made it. Then I asked to see it. Holy Crap, Brielle. You..." He grinned. "You made a freaking Celestial orb."

My lips curved into a smile too. I couldn't help it; his dimples made the happiness come out of me. "I know. It was awesome, and scary, *and* pretty much awesome."

Lincoln's fingers reached out, stroking my cheek. "But you're tired?" he asked, concern filling his voice.

My hand waved in nonchalance. "Mr. Rincor said it's normal after releasing so much light."

His brow furrowed, but then he nodded. "Come on. I have a little surprise for you."

A surprise? I had a love-hate relationship with surprises. On one hand, I loved them and the spontaneity of it all, while on the other hand, my inner control freak wanted to know everything.

Lincoln stepped into the apartment and waved

me in. As I gingerly crossed the threshold, I noticed that Chloe and her brother Donnie were there, which Luke was totally freaking out about, I was sure. The Beast Shifter was lingering in the corner of the dining room, staring at Donnie wistfully.

Everyone was standing around Noah and Darren, who were sitting at the dining table gesturing to something.

The apartment was nice from what I'd seen so far. Blandly furnished with tans and grays, but clean and updated. Lincoln's hand wrapped around mine, as he led me over to the table.

"Where's Blake?" I asked, noticing one member was missing from the usual foursome. Just then, he emerged from the bathroom.

"The gang's all here!" Lincoln declared, clapping Blake on the back. "Let's get started."

I frowned. "I thought this was a housewarming party. What's going on?" Lincoln was most definitely acting shady.

The crowd parted, and I finally saw what was on the table—a bunch of maps and papers.

My boyfriend gestured to the crowd. "We can't imagine what's it's like to be without your infinity weapon, so we've gathered tonight to make a plan to help you get Sera back."

Hope burst inside my chest as my throat tightened. "For real? You think we can get her back?"

Donnie stepped forward. "I spoke to a friend,

another Nightblood, who once lost his infinity weapon in a portal. He's a commander in the Fallen Army now."

My heart was jackknifing in my chest. "Okay."

Donnie gave me a handsome grin, and I swear Luke melted into a puddle in the corner.

"So, what he did was to go back to the same spot he lost it in, and open a new portal. Then he had a Light Mage amplify his connection with the weapon, and use a powerful retrieving spell to get it back for him."

"Oh my God! Can we do that?" I asked Lincoln. If he said no, I was doing it anyway. I needed Sera back no matter what.

He gave a hesitant nod. "We can, but there's more to it."

"While they were retrieving the weapon, a few demons got through and...someone died," Donnie continued, ending on a barely audible whisper.

A dark storm cloud floated over my rainbows of bliss.

"Oh."

Lincoln's fingers threaded through mine. "You lost Sera in Inferno, so it's not exactly the best location, but we're going to make a plan and give it a try."

I nodded, knowing that was all I could really hope for.

"Because we all know you can't pass Fight Night without her," Noah teased.

I pinned my healing teacher with a glare. "Says the guy who spends forty-five minutes on his hair every morning."

The group erupted into a collective "Ohhh." The shit-talking had commenced.

"Open some beers. It's going to be a long night." Lincoln instructed.

We settled into the plan. Of course, Shea was going to be my Light Mage helper, since she was a master at opening and closing portals now. She'd been working with Mr. Claymore in her free time, and was fully confident she could do this for me.

"I'm working an op tomorrow night in Inferno. I could get you guys clearance as a watch team," Blake offered us.

"A watch team?" I inquired.

"Second years can go into the war zones when it's not their assigned night, and do a watch night. They basically shadow a mission," he explained.

My heart beat faster. "Yes, let's do that."

Lincoln whistled. "We're going to pull this together in one night?"

Shea slammed her fist onto the table. "Hell yeah, we are!" she blurted out, a mild slur in her voice.

Lincoln raised one eyebrow at Noah. "Let's cut Shea off, okay?"

She'd had like two beers. Lightweight.

Noah chuckled, rubbing the top of Shea's head and messing up her curly hair. "I'll make her my famous waffles while you guys plan our team. We're going to need at least half a dozen soldiers, preferably more in case something scary comes through the portal."

Shea shot Noah a death glare, and I knew it was because he'd messed up her hair. You *never* touched a woman's curls. I knew from living with Shea the past six years, that there was no way back from a perfect curl turning to floofy frizz. You had to re-wet it to get that tight tendril look again, and Shea was not one to spend that much time on it twice in one day.

Shea smoothed her locks as best she could and motioned to Donnie. "Can you make it tomorrow?"

"Absolutely," he answered with a nod. "I can bring three of my buddies."

Grabbing a piece of paper and a pen, Shea started to make a list. From the sight of her handwriting, she was definitely tipsy.

Donnie turned to my gay bestie, then. "Luke, you game for tomorrow night? Could really use a big strong shifter."

Luke's mouth hung open a little, beer clutched tightly in his hand. He wasn't saying anything. *Wow, I think the words 'big strong shifter' coming from Donnie's lips froze his brain.*

"He's game. Totally," Chloe interjected for Luke, which seemed to snap him out of his love trance.

"Totally." Luke's voice cracked a little, and Donnie smiled wider.

Oh my God, they're so cute. It was obvious to everyone that Luke was crushing on Donnie, and Donnie didn't seem to mind one bit. *Interesting.*

"Cool. Noah and I can work on finding a few more, but I think we've got a solid team. There's no way we can let a seraph blade go that easily," Lincoln stated next to me.

It had been three weeks. Twenty-something days without her. She was just lying there alone, or already in the hands of someone new. What if I didn't find her?

Fatigue slammed into me then. It was nighttime now, and my three-hour nap had done nothing to help me recover from my magical antics.

"I'm exhausted." I swayed on my feet.

Lincoln's brow knit with concern. "Noah, can you scan her?" Grasping each of my shoulders, he started to nudge me toward the bedroom. "Sleep over. You need rest," he whispered.

Shea and I had come together, but apparently she was going to be sleeping at Noah's, who was only a few apartments away, so I figured it would be all right. All my brain could focus on at that point was the idea of sleep, regardless of where it happened.

I let him lead me into the bedroom, and gave a lopsided smile at the familiar denim bedding from his trailer.

"Hey, I thought this was a two-bedroom. What you gonna do with the second one?" I kicked off my shoes as he pulled the blanket back.

His dark hair was tousled over his forehead, making his blue eyes pop. "I was thinking of an office or a music room. Start collecting guitars."

A grin curved my lips. "Definitely a music room. With a little corner for your poetry books," I teased.

He poked me in the rib cage, and I fell onto the bed in a fit of laughter. I was so exhausted it was like being drunk.

"You said you were going to let that go," he told me with mock hurt. My man was crazy for poetry, and I loved it.

"I love you," I remarked, looking up at him.

Noah peeked over his shoulder then. "Aw, I love you too."

I could no longer keep my eyes open, so I just smiled in response, and let them close.

"She's never been this tired before, not even when I tried to kill her in boot camp," Lincoln explained to the healer.

"Heard that," I mumbled.

"Dude, she produced a freaking Celestial orb. That takes nearly all the light we carry. She just needs rest." Noah's voice was lighthearted; he clearly wasn't concerned.

"Just scan her, bro. I'm serious," Lincoln urged him firmly.

"Fine." Noah's voice was clipped.

I felt it then, the warm buzz of Noah's energy, scanning down my back.

The bed was so comfortable, my body melted into it as I drifted off to sleep.

"Oh... Interesting." Noah's words were all I heard before I hit dreamland.

CHAPTER 11

I AWOKE FEELING REFRESHED, AND ROLLED OVER to see the clock said it was noon.

Oh my God! I overslept.

I sat upright and looked for Lincoln, but instead, I found a piece of paper with his small block letter handwriting on it.

HAD TO SEE RAPH ABOUT SOMETHING. WANTED TO LET YOU SLEEP. FOOD IS IN THE FRIDGE.
LOVE YOU.
LINC
PS: YOU SNORED LIKE A TRAIN LAST NIGHT.

I smiled at the letter. It was so Lincoln.

Pulling myself out of bed, I quickly showered, and totally swooned when I saw Lincoln had transferred my pink toothbrush from the trailer to his new place. He'd even kept some of my clothes in his top drawer. I changed quickly, and then poured some cereal into a large bowl. Cereal for lunch was totally my favorite thing.

I texted Shea that I was awake, and there was a knock at the door thirty seconds later.

"I totally didn't get laid," she exclaimed, barging past me.

I snorted. "What?"

"After all that sex Olympics talk, he rejected me. Said I'd been drinking and he wanted our first time to be special," Shea declared with a frown, as if a special night of sex with Noah was the worst thing in the world.

I chuckled. "Okay, and what's wrong with that? He's being a total gentleman."

My bestie was wearing Noah's shirt, which hung halfway down her legs, and her wild curly hair was in two puffball pigtails. She looked adorable.

"I know. Maybe I misjudged him." She collapsed onto Lincoln's couch dramatically, like she was auditioning for a daytime soap opera.

"Ya think?" I managed through my cereal-stuffed mouth.

She sat up, fully erect as shock marred her face. "Oh my God."

Panic seized me. "What's wrong?"

"I'm totally in love with him," she declared.

I smacked my forehead and decided to drop the subject. Shea was utterly clueless when it came to all things Noah.

"How crazy was Luke last night, gushing over Donnie?" I asked, choosing to switch gears.

Shea laughed. "Oh my God, I thought Luke was going to start humping his leg. So cute and sad."

I nodded with a smile, but then my mind shifted to more important topics. "You ready for tonight?"

I needed Sera back. She was an extension of my soul, so being without her was physically painful at that point. I felt half-empty inside.

Shea's face took on a look of determination. "Totally. We'll get her back. Don't worry."

My phone buzzed then, and I nearly yelped when I saw it was Clark.

I scrambled to grab it, and mashed the green button to accept the call.

"Hey, any news on my brother?" My voice was frantic. He'd said to give him another week. It had only been a day. Something had to be wrong.

"Hey, Bri." Mikey's voice flared through the phone instead; it had dropped three octaves and was hoarse.

Relief flooded my entire body and I burst into tears. I hadn't heard his voice in over a month. Part of me thought I might never hear it again. Shea rushed from the couch to sit with me as I tried to find my own voice.

"You're okay?" I finally managed.

"I'll be okay. Yeah."

"Have you called Mom?" My poor mother was worried sick over the whole situation. Not being able to talk to, or see him was torturing her.

"Yeah. She's coming to see me tomorrow. Clark says it's safe," Mikey confirmed.

I swallowed. "Well I'm free this afternoon. Shea and I will come right now."

"Tomorrow is best," Clark's voice broke in, and I groaned. This alpha was a real piece of work. Talk about control freak, but he'd gotten my brother back, so I couldn't complain.

"Tomorrow's fine," I agreed.

My thoughts were going a mile a minute. Did Clark take my brother's wolf to the cemetery to see my dad? Had that healed him somehow? I didn't want to ask and trigger anything, but I really wanted to know at some point.

"Love you, Bri. Gotta go," Mikey breathed.

The tears were back. "I love you too. Even though you annoy me all the time, I freaking love you, Mikey. Okay?"

"Okay." I could hear the smile in his voice.

After I hung up, Shea just held me as I laughed, and cried happy tears.

My brother was going to be okay. Now I just

needed to get Sera, win Fight Night, and buy my mom's contract.

I would get her out of Demon City. I had to. It's what my dad would have wanted.

———·———

Night had fallen, and we'd been granted shadow passes to tag along on Blake's mission with his team. But little did the Fallen Army leaders know, we were going to split off, and retrieve my infinity weapon.

After passing through the military checkpoint at the edge of Angel City, Lincoln checked in with Blake, and we set a rendezvous point to meet up after we'd gotten Sera back. Now we were all in a bus, a dozen of us including Chloe, Donnie, Luke, Noah, Darren, Shea, and some of their trusted army buddies, one of whom was a powerful Light Mage named Nora. Her hair was as white as cotton, but she looked way too young for it to be natural.

I was touched that everyone had come together on my account. Okay, maybe they'd come because my boyfriend was a lieutenant, well-loved member of the army, and Sera was a seraph blade currently stuck in Hell, but whatever. They were here—that was all that mattered.

We drove in silence to the apartment building where I'd seen my first, and hopefully last, Succubus demon.

I shivered a little, thinking about what she'd looked like, especially those sunken pits for eyes.

Before I knew it, we'd pulled into a parallel parking spot at the front curb. My mind went back to that night, and what I'd learned recently in my history class.

"Hey, Lincoln," I whispered.

My lover was in a conversation with Donnie. After looking over at me, he wrapped it up, then came to sit by me. "What's up? You ready? Feeling okay?"

I nodded, tightening the steel cuffs that he'd given me around my arms. "I was just thinking. If Sera was thrown into the portal on the second floor, and the underworld is directly underneath us, then should we open the portal on the bottom floor? So I can search the ground in Hell?"

Yes, I just had a normal conversation about opening a portal to Hell.

Lincoln nodded, thinking. "That's actually a good plan, but it gives us a higher chance of something coming through since we'll be at their ground level. That Succubus could have dropped Sera in the middle of a Demon City in hell for all we know."

There were Demon Cities in hell! Of course there were. Then she'd probably been stolen. All I'd seen before that portal closed was a hazy red sky, and then Sera was gone.

"I think it's our best shot," I told him.

He stared at his hand a moment and then nodded. "All right. Let's do it."

After relaying the slight change in plans, our team embarked on the journey.

Nerves were tightly grabbing hold of me as we walked over to the apartment door directly below the one I'd lost Sera in that night.

Lincoln banged on the door loudly and it creaked open, the handle missing.

He stepped inside, lighting the way with the scope on top of his weapon. "Fallen Army, anyone here?" he shouted.

Noah went in behind him and they both did a quick sweep. When they returned, they beckoned us inside.

"Abandoned. Looks like Snakeroot demons used to live here. Everything is acid-charred, so watch your step," Lincoln called out into the hallway where we stood on standby.

As I stepped forward, I felt total and complete hope that I would find Sera, and that scared me. If I didn't, I was going to be crushed.

Nora, the Light Mage, approached Shea as we stepped into the living room. "You've opened a Hell portal before?" she asked skeptically, no doubt eyeing my second-year best friend like a newbie.

Shea was anything but humble. That's where she and Noah were perfect for each other.

"I've mastered it. Trust me, I can open and close

this thing in sixty seconds if need be." Shea propped one hand on her hip for snarky emphasis.

The Light Mage held her hands up defensively. "All right. I'll ready the spell to amplify your connection to the weapon, Brielle, and then we can do the retrieval spell. But first, I need some of your blood to tap into the energy you share with the weapon."

My eyes bugged a little. What was it with these people and wanting blood samples?

"The retrieval spell might not be necessary. I've learned how to call my weapon from far away from Archangel Michael," I told her.

She nodded. "We can try it, but just know that down there, everything is different. Trust me." The expression in her face told me she'd been through something, and I should trust her.

I simply nodded, handing her my finger.

Lincoln was right beside me the entire time as the rest of our group fanned out to protect us. Half were ordered to focus on outside threats here in Inferno, while the other half of our team had to protect us from anything that might try to come out of the portal.

The sound of cracking bones pulled my attention but I didn't even bother to look over, knowing it was Luke shifting back to human form.

As Nora sliced my finger, my blood dripped onto a purple crystal. "Is it true you can talk to the weapon? Like a true mental connection?" she asked.

Up close, her face had fine lines around the eyes, and I thought she might be a bit older than she looked. I also wondered what had turned her hair white, or if she'd been born with that unique shade.

I nodded in response to her question, and she started to move her hands in an intricate pattern. Purple shafts of light shot out, wrapping around the crystal.

"This should restore that. You might be able to speak to her again, if she's close by," the Light Mage declared.

I nearly wept at her words. I knew everyone there had a soul weapon, and they were all bound to it, so they should know how I felt, but I also didn't think anyone had a connection quite like Sera and I did.

The purple light intensified, and Nora looked at my necklace. "That thing reeks of magic. You'll need to take it off, or it'll interfere with my spell."

"Sure." I started to unclasp it, but Lincoln thrust a hand out to stop me.

"I don't think that's a good idea," he added softly.

"Why not?" I pressed him.

His hand pushed through his hair. "Because…"

"Your light energy has the upper hand right now," Noah said what Lincoln clearly couldn't. "If you take it off, you might allow your…dark gifts to emerge even stronger, and push the light back even further."

"What!" I shouted.

"Guys, this spell has a time stamp!" Nora

growled, holding the purple crystal out to me. It was glowing and swirling, and in that moment, I couldn't even process what the boys had said.

My glare cut into Lincoln and he winced. "Last night, Noah scanned you and discovered that, so...I don't know if it's worth it, Bri."

Screw that. Sera was family just as much as Shea or my mom was.

Reaching up, I unclipped the necklace. "She's worth it. I'd do the same for you," I informed him curtly.

His face fell as I set the necklace into his hand.

The moment my fingers released the chain, I felt a surge of energy buzz up along my spine and wrap around my heart, pinching it in a viselike grip. I gasped, short of breath for a moment.

Lincoln stepped closer, pressing in on me. "Oh God, what's wrong?"

I glared at him, then slowly turned to stare at all of them. "I'm going to kill you all." Venom dripped from my voice.

One by one, their faces dropped. Noah actually took a step back.

I couldn't hold it in any longer. Laughter burst out of me and I keeled forward, holding my stomach.

"Something's not right with her," Nora told the room.

Lincoln's chest fell as he sighed in relief. "That wasn't funny."

Shea snickered. "It kind of was."

"Are we doing this or not?" Nora snapped, holding the glowing crystal in her hand.

I nodded. Whatever weirdness I'd felt when I took the necklace off was gone now.

I was getting Sera no matter what.

"I'm fine. I feel fine. It's all good. Let's do this." I tried to push reassurance into my voice, but Lincoln's face still held concern.

Shea started to work on the portal as Nora took two paces toward me. "This might hurt a bit," she declared and then slammed the crystal onto my chest, right over my tattoo.

Pain flared to life where the crystal touched me, and then a massive headache rocked my world. My hands flew to my skull as I moaned.

"Why?" I grunted.

Nora released the crystal; the purple magic had left the rock, and was now dancing around my body in whirls. "It's reconnecting your bond, which was somewhat severed when your weapon was tossed into another realm," she informed me.

Lincoln's hand came up to rub my back, and I tried to work through the ice pick that was stabbing my brain.

I was just about to ask how long it would last when the pain lessened, and I heard something.

'Bri!'

Joy ripped through my body as I nearly cried in relief. *'Sera! I'm here!'* I told her.

133

"The portal is almost ready," Shea stated.

"I'm talking to her!" I shouted.

A few raised their eyebrows, but I didn't care if I looked crazy. I was freaking talking to Sera! I hadn't realized how lonely I was for her companionship, until I heard her voice in my head.

'It's bad down here. Everything smells awful,' Sera lamented.

Laughter bubbled up in my chest, and now I was really getting some crazy looks, even from Lincoln.

'You don't have a nose,' I reminded her.

Shea had started to open the portal. As she did, I saw a desolate landscape come into view.

Oh God.

I'd never peered into Hell. I mean, the one time Shea opened the portal in the training room, it was in the floor and I'd been too focused on the demons crawling out to notice anything. Then when Lucifer came through, he'd done so within a building, so I'd only seen a wall. The Succubus had opened one in the sky and all I'd seen was smoke, but this...this was my first view of Hell in all its horrific nature.

'Where are you?' I breathed as my eyes swept over the hordes of demons that passed before us. We seemed to be in some alleyway between two crumbling buildings, and the stench of sulfur and oil was nauseating.

'I'm a cactus,' she exclaimed.

My brow burrowed. *'Excuse me?'*

Was she drunk? Was it possible for her to get drunk? She could smell, so probably.

Maybe I was drunk.

'I've been using all my power to morph myself into a cactus, so one of these cesspools doesn't pick me up and sell me.'

My eyes widened. *'You can do that?'*

'Hurry, I can't hold it much longer. I'd nearly given up hope.'

For three weeks she's been draining her magic to appear as a cactus?

I needed to focus before one of the passing demons noticed us. I couldn't see any cacti nearby, but I figured Michael's retrieval spell would still work.

Taking a deep breath, I felt for Sera's energy, but nothing happened.

'I can't feel you,' I told her with panic.

'I don't think that will work here.'

"Can you do the retrieval spell?" I asked the Light Mage, who seemed lost in concentration.

Nora growled and shook her head. "It's not working. Her energy is different. You're going to have to call her to you."

Dammit. Could it be because she was a cactus? But if she dropped her illusion and was suddenly a shiny dagger on the ground, the demons might pick her up.

I closed my eyes and tried again, pulling at my

Celestial magic, which felt a thousand miles away right then.

Then realization hit me in the gut. My Sera retrieval was a Celestial light gift, and when I'd taken off my necklace, it had forced the darkness to rear up.

'I...*can't feel you. I can't call to you,*' I explained.

'*Do you see the burning building?*' she asked.

My eyes flicked to the sky. Off to the left about thirty feet was a smoke stack. '*I think so.*'

'*There's a street fight going on right now. The demons fight here all the time. I'm right in front of the burning building. If you're quick, you can sneak in and grab me. They shouldn't notice you.*'

Go in? Did my infinity weapon just suggest I step into Hell and get her?

She's totally drunk.

That thought had never crossed my mind, that I would enter and get her, not to mention Lincoln would never allow it. It bothered me that I couldn't see Sera. What if this was Lucifer's trick, and her voice in my head wasn't real?

'*How did I feel about Lincoln when I first met him?*' I asked her.

I could almost sense a smile in her, if that were possible. '*You hated his guts, and you stole his fruit, yet you secretly wanted to see him naked.*'

I burst out laughing, and now Lincoln was really looking at me with concern.

"I need your sword." I peered at my lover. "She needs to feel another soul weapon so she can guide herself to that," I lied.

If I died, he'd never forgive me. I knew from history class that he couldn't follow me in, but I was pretty sure I'd be able to walk through that hole, and I was also pretty sure my best friend wasn't going to let me go in alone. Even now, Shea was watching me like a hawk.

He pulled his sword without hesitation and handed it to me.

I wrapped my fingers around the cold steel and gave him a weak smile.

Forgive me.

CHAPTER 12

I KNEW IF I WALKED SLOWLY TOWARD THE OPENING, Lincoln might grab me, so I lunged, darting so quickly that I heard the room take a collective gasp. The moment I crossed into the dark realm, a weight pushed on my skin, and for a moment it became more difficult to breathe.

Spinning, I noticed that just as I anticipated, Shea was right behind me.

"Get back here!" Lincoln whisper-screamed, eyes wide as saucers as he gaped at me from the living room where he stood.

Shea was panting, sweat beading on her forehead.

"This is the only way. I'll be right back. She's not far," I assured him.

"No!" Lincoln hissed. He reached one hand

into the portal, then recoiled so quickly you'd have thought he was burned. A strangled yelp fled his throat, and I stepped closer to him.

"Are you okay?" It was weird to see an opening into another world.

He held up his arm to reveal a horrible bruise. Some parts of his skin were torn and bleeding.

Oh God.

We needed to be quick.

"I'll be right back!" I promised.

Nora took off her cloak, and chucked it through the portal at my feet. "You're an idiot," she stated.

Okay, not really a necessary comment, but whatever.

Pulling the cloak from the dusty ground, I quickly swung it over my shoulders, hiding Lincoln's sword underneath and pulling the hood over my head.

"If you're not back here in three minutes, I'm coming in," Lincoln declared.

Considering what it did to his arm, that would probably kill him.

'*We're coming,*' I told Sera.

I didn't waste time, only nodded and grabbed Shea's hand with my free one as we both started to power-walk down the alley.

"She's disguised as a cactus and is in front of the building that's on fire. There's a street fight, so we should be able to slip in and out." I caught Shea up to speed.

As we neared the end of the alley, we both stopped dead.

Holy mother of Hell.

The scene before me was a total culture shock. I couldn't even process my own thoughts about it.

Other than the demons milling about and fighting off to the right like Sera said they were, there were souls. Spectral humanlike creatures walking around and wincing fearfully every time a demon neared them. One of them was a sweet-looking old lady.

What the...?

Shea snapped out of it before I did, and jerked my hand to the left, where a dilapidated building was on fire. I took quick strides in the direction of the flaming structure. What I'd seen so far shook me to my core, but I had to stay focused. The roads weren't paved, but I was shocked to see that we seemed to be in some sort of city. The demons were fighting in front of what looked like a store, where someone was handing out food baskets from an open window.

The sweet old lady soul suddenly dropped to the ground and started screaming bloody murder.

Shit. What's going on in this place?

The closer we moved to the burning building, the hotter I became.

There, five feet from me, was a tiny barrel cactus half covered in soot and dirt. Finally I could feel her.

'I'm here,' I thought, and in that moment she dropped her illusion, changing her form.

In one swift move, I scooped down and picked her up. The moment the cold steel hit my hand, a wave of love poured through me, chasing the darkness back.

Sera was my light. She was an extension of my soul, the lightest part of me. I could feel that now. Tears pricked my eyes as I clutched her to my chest.

'*I missed you so much,*' I told her.

'*Me too. You smell good, like home.*'

A smile curved my lips, but the smirk quickly died when Shea elbowed my rib cage hard.

I spun slowly to see a Snakeroot demon staring at us.

"Earth dwellers," he hissed in a tiny rat chirpy voice, pointing to us.

They can speak?

I put my finger to my lips, as if the act of asking him to keep it a secret would work. The mob—which I now realized was fighting over food—had grown, and I didn't want to know what would happen if they knew we were there.

Snakeroot demons loved candy, and I happened to have a pack of mint gum in my pocket. I slowly handed Shea Lincoln's sword and reached for the gum.

"You want some candy?" I whispered.

Desire flared in his eyes. He looked emaciated, not like the Snakeroot demons I knew on Earth.

With one nod, he crouched as if ready to pounce on me.

141

I quickly ripped open the flap to the gum and tossed a piece on the floor.

He lunged for it and ate it in one bite, the metallic wrapper included. His nostrils flared as his eyes landed on the packet in my hands.

I tossed another piece as Shea and I started to inch backward toward the alley.

"We gotta start keeping more candy on us," Shea whispered.

"Agreed." *You never know when you'll run into a hungry Snakeroot demon.*

I kept throwing pieces of gum in front of him, but he was inhaling them like he hadn't eaten in weeks. And now a few of the other demons in the mob had trickled away and were smelling the air.

Freaking mint. Or human. I didn't know which it was, but they were totally staring at us, so they'd smelled something off. *Why can't Hell have mint? It should be a normal thing.*

"Time to run." I gulped and chucked the whole packet. Shea handed Lincoln's sword to me and I pivoted, kicking off the dusty ground into a full-on sprint with my bestie right behind me.

"I'm going to start closing the portal!" she shouted, her hands making wide arcs in the air as purple magic danced about in her palms.

Unfortunately, there was a Castor demon gunning for me, and I knew I wouldn't make it to the portal in time without a fight.

'*I don't have much strength left,*' Sera told me.

I'd figured, which was why I'd brought Lincoln's weapon. It may not have been my own soul weapon, but it was still a big-ass sword, and I was hoping since it was tied to Lincoln's soul, it would help me.

Just as we reached the mouth of the alley, I spun.

The Castor demon was right on me. With one thrust of his gnarled hands, he shot an energy pulse straight at my gut. I held Lincoln's sword before me and it deflected some of the blast, but I was still rocked backward.

"Bri!" Lincoln's strangled voice cut through the space and filtered down the alleyway. He must have had a view of what was going on, but I didn't have time to focus on him.

Shea was there then, throwing a purple ball of energy at the ugly Castor demon. It crashed into his chest and he faltered, tipping his head back to roar.

I turned when I heard movement behind me. The sound of their comrade in trouble had alerted the mob.

Shit.

'*Run.*' Sera was stating the obvious, but damn, it was good to have her voice back in my head.

Shea hooked me under the armpit and hauled me up just as the Castor demon lunged for me. Castor demons, aside from throwing mini EMP bursts at you, had nearly impenetrable skin—except behind their heels. Don't ask me how I knew that; long story short, it was Shea's fault.

"Start closing the portal. I'll jump through!" I told her.

No way was I going to let this angry mob through to kill my friends and loved ones. The friends who'd helped me get Sera back.

"Fine!" Shea snapped, clearly not happy with my plan.

There was no time to dwell on it.

I shook Lincoln's sword a little. "Come on. Go blue," I urged it. I'd seen Lincoln do the blinding blue light thing a million times, and if this sword was an intelligent being, then maybe—

Blue light flared to life along the blade, and I ran to meet the Castor demon head-on. Lincoln's sword was in my left hand, Sera in my right. As I suspected, when I made it within two feet of the demon, he flared out with a burst of energy. With a cry, I held up Lincoln's sword and it acted as a shield, the blue light breaking apart the energy burst.

I didn't want to give him time to build another, so I dropped to my knees and slashed out, prison style, with Sera's short and sharp blade. I made short fast hacks into the back of his right heel, and he went down with a roar. Tucking my head in, I rolled to the side, hitting the wall of the alley to avoid getting smooshed by the demon.

The crowd was on us now, though the other demons were slightly shocked by the Castor demon falling over in a flood of black blood.

"Come on!" Shea yelled.

Bursting from the ground and yanking Lincoln's heavy-ass sword up in front of me, I took off running.

The portal was about a three-foot circle now, beyond it was Lincoln's pissed-off face, and a pile of cushions—to ease my landing, I guessed.

Those blue eyes were livid. Oops. For two people in love, I sure made him mad a lot.

Hot acid hit the back of my calf and I faltered, pain flaring to life just below my knee. My all-out run turned to a frantic limp.

The blood drained from Lincoln's face and he pulled a gun. "Jump!" he shouted, raising the weapon.

Oh God. What's behind me?

Having your boyfriend point a gun at you—even if it wasn't directly *at* you—was not cool, but I leaped off the crusted ground with my good leg, tucking the weapons into my body in a way that wouldn't gore me when I landed.

As I sailed through the space, Lincoln popped off multiple shots, shooting over my head and into the hole. I hit the pile of cushions with a crash, the wind still knocked out of me as I let the weapons fall away from my body.

Loud yells and grunts rose up behind me, and I rolled off the pile of pillows to see the shrinking portal and the group of angry demons beyond it. My freaking calf muscle was on fire, but I knew better than to complain—if I did, Lincoln would probably shoot me.

One more stream of acid shot through the opening, and we all scrambled out of the way to dodge it. Then, the portal closed.

Slowly, every single person turned to look in my direction.

I held up Sera. "Got it." I gave a nervous laugh.

Lincoln slowly stalked toward me, jaw clenched, eyes on me like a predator, and I knew in that moment that he was pissed as all hell. He leaned down to me and my heart thumped, but instead of helping me up, he reached for his blade and stood, sliding it into his sheath.

"Heal her leg," he barked at Noah, then spun on his heel and left the room.

'He's mad at you. Like really mad at you.' Sera's voice, however annoying sometimes, was a welcome sound in my head. Just not right then.

'Your knowledge of human emotions astounds me,' I informed her.

'Ew, sarcasm,' Sera hissed.

Noah reached down and did help me up. "Let's see what we're dealing with."

I looked at Shea, sweat still beading on her forehead, and reached for her hand. "You okay?"

She nodded, holding her stomach. "Just feel a bit ill. That place…it was hard to be there."

"Yeah," I lied. But it hadn't been hard. It had felt a bit…heavy, but once I got used to it, I was fine.

Oh God, what's wrong with me?

CHAPTER 13

LINCOLN IGNORED ME ON THE BUS RIDE BACK INTO Angel City, and it had me feeling like shit. I had to go in there or I never would have gotten Sera back. Yes, it was reckless, but it had all worked out in the end.

Finally, as the bus approached the school, Lincoln walked to the back row, where I was sitting alone, and slid next to me. Shea had intentionally left it open in hopes that he would.

He sat rigid, face forward. "How's your leg?" he asked.

My heart melted a little at his concern. "Burns a lot, but at least it's not bleeding anymore. Noah said it'll scar."

Lincoln nodded curtly, finally turning to look at me. "You sleeping over?"

It was a weekend. I always slept over on weekends. I had my Sunday family thing with Mikey and my mom the following day, but that didn't mean I couldn't sleep over.

"You're pissed at me, so why do you want me to sleep over?" I hit him with the obvious truth.

He smirked a little. "Because I also love you, and I'm concerned about your leg—*and* your sanity—so I want to keep an eye on you. I'll be sleeping on the couch."

"Oh." That hurt. Not the sanity part, because he said stuff like that all the time—that was actually our way of flirting, verbal jabs—but the part about sleeping on the couch hurt.

Still, I couldn't say no. I needed to repair this between us. He was everything to me.

"Yeah. I'll sleep over." My voice was barely a whisper, but it was enough to be heard as he nodded again.

After the bus pulled up to the school, Lincoln thanked them all, and declared the mission a success. But I could see behind that fake glassy smile. He was so pissed, and I was surprised he hadn't exploded on me yet.

I sensed a verbal ass-kicking when we got back to his place.

Sure enough, the moment he closed the door behind us, he spun on me. "Just tell me why. Why do you always put yourself in these life-threatening situations? Are you suicidal?"

That hurt. As someone who'd had dark thoughts every once in a while, I knew you didn't just scream, "Are you suicidal?" in someone's face.

"No. I love my life. I love you. But I love my family too. Shea was worth the risk. Mikey is worth the risk. My mother will be worth the risk. Sera—"

"Sera is a fucking knife!" He cut me off with a strangled yell.

'I resent that,' Sera said from my hip. I tried to ignore her.

"Yeah, she is to you, but she's special to me. I love her, and I know that sounds crazy, but I also need her to free my mom. I'm powerful, but I'm not *that* powerful. I need her to protect my family. I made a risky call and I'm sorry. I didn't grow up in Beverly Hills, with golden sunrays filtering through the breakfast window every morning, as we sat around and talked about angels. I'm from the hood, Lincoln!" I screamed, my hands shaking. "In the hood, we learn to survive at all costs. We take risks because they present themselves every day, and in my life? Family. Comes. *First*."

I swear to God, if he challenged me, I would somehow breathe fire into his face, I was that livid.

His face fell. "What about me? Am I your family?"

And just like that, the wind fell from my sails and I was falling. Tears pricked my vision as I stepped closer to him. "Of course you are. You're... I love you so much it hurts," I told him.

He looked off at a blank wall. "And if you had gone into Hell tonight and hadn't come back, do you know what that would have done to me? Knowing I couldn't go after you? It would have *killed* me. I'd be dead."

A huge gaping hole opened in my chest as his words slammed into me. I was his family. His only family.

"I'm sorry." Okay, fine, I probably should have started with that.

He nodded and pulled me into his arms. His chin came over the top of my head, and I felt his warm breath coat my hair. "I can't go through loss again. You understand?"

I did. I did it once with my father and I couldn't do it again either.

I nodded. "I'm exhausted." Pulling back, I met his eyes.

He glanced at the couch. "I'm just gonna watch some TV and crash out here. I need to shake this off."

With a frown, I shook my head and shuffled into the bedroom to run a bath. Careful not to get my healing skin wet, I washed up quickly and brushed my teeth, slipping into bed. Lying there, lonely and unsure, I couldn't fall asleep until 12:36 am. That was the moment Lincoln crept in, and slipped beside me, tucking me into his body.

The second my back rested against his warm chest, a contented sigh escaped me.

"I have plans for us, Brielle, and in order to enjoy them, you need to be alive," he whispered into my hair.

I was too tired to respond, so I just nodded and drifted off to sleep.

———•———

Once I picked up my mother from Demon City, I drove us both out to Clark's land. It was far, like almost into the war zone far, but still within Angel City. We'd been instructed to wear bright-colored clothing, and stay in our vehicle until Clark came out to greet us. I didn't want to know why, I just wanted to see my brother. We'd also been instructed not to hug or touch Mikey unless he initiated physical contact. He was still fighting his urge to hunt, apparently. Another thing I really didn't want to know about.

"My poor baby, living out in the woods like an animal," my mother bemoaned as I drove up the long dirt driveway to Clark's property.

"Well, he *is* an animal, Mom, and Clark was able to help him, so I think this is the best place for him," I told her.

My brother was a wolf, my mom raised the dead, and I was Lucifer's abomination. My family was messed up, but I'd just learned to accept it—unlike my mother.

She sighed. "Don't hug him. That alpha man said not to hug my own son!"

That 'alpha man' is trying to save you from getting your head chewed off, I wanted to say, but thought better of it.

"It's temporary, Mom. Once he gets full control, he'll be at school with me, and then recruited into the army, making a good living."

She nodded but was rubbing her palms against her jeans, which was her nervous gesture.

We passed a thicket of trees and then a house came into view. A group of houses, actually, all a mere ten feet apart.

"They live like a little cult," my mom said, already judging the place.

I rolled my eyes. "Mom," I warned in my big girl voice.

She shooed me away with one hand. "Fine. I'll be open-minded."

I nodded. That was all I'd asked of her before embarking on this trip.

I pulled up to the biggest house, assuming the alpha would take that, and put the car in park. Within seconds, the front door opened and Clark walked out, my brother was right behind him, next to some pretty black-haired girl. She looked my age but had a maturity about her.

As my brother came closer, I noticed he looked like he'd been on steroids or something. He was a beefcake now, and I really wanted to tease him about it but wouldn't. At least not right away.

"All right, let's get out." I opened the door.

We stepped out gingerly, awkwardly standing before my brother as he stared at us with a pained smile.

"Hey, Mikey. Glad to see you not so furry," I joked.

That caused him to smile, which showcased two large canine teeth pressing down on his bottom lip.

My mom gasped a little and covered it with an awkward cough. Mikey made no move to hug us, which hurt, but I understood he was dealing with some demons.

"I missed you," Mom murmured.

He nodded. "Me too, Mom."

Clark looked at the black-haired girl and nodded, before walking away without a word.

Weirdo.

"Doing okay?" the black-haired girl asked.

Mikey gave her a short nod. "This is Elise."

She stepped forward and extended her hand. "I'm Michael's sponsor. I help him...get acquainted." She shook my mother's hand, then mine.

My mom gave me one raised eyebrow. I knew the

word 'sponsor' had her thinking of an alcoholic.

"Let's sit." Elise pointed at a picnic table that was off to the side of Clark's house.

"Do you like it here?" Mom asked him, looking at Elise as if she didn't trust her.

Mikey smiled, once again shocking me with those big teeth. "Yeah. It was a rough time at first, but now that I'm able to hold my human form, we play a lot of games. I'm really good at foosball."

Elise smiled. "You're okay."

He gave her a sheepish look. Yeah, they were totally into each other.

"How old are you?" I blurted out to her.

Her eyes met mine, and for the slightest second, they flashed orange. "Twenty."

Hmm, same age as me. I decided to be civil and change the subject. "So, I heard you'll be starting classes in the fall?"

Just then, a twig snapped, and Mikey's head shot to the thick woods that lined the property. He took a slow, deep inhale, flexing his nostrils, as his eyes turned the color of honey. My hand went to the blade on my thigh and my mother leaned into me.

Elise's entire body was clenched, as if she were ready to take Mikey to the ground if need be.

"There's a rabbit nearby," Mikey said.

Elise nodded. "Do you want to go hunting?"

Mikey shook his head. "I think my mom and sister should leave."

Without another word, Elise burst from the table and rushed my mom and me into our car, telling us to lock the doors. I was in total shock that my shithead little brother, whom I'd always teased and thought of as a punk, was some dangerous beast now.

"It'll be okay," I lied to my mom.

She didn't say a word, just cried the whole way home.

Maybe this was Mikey's life now, only able to live with his pack to control his beast. If that was the case, then I had to be okay with it. It wasn't exactly what I had envisioned for our family, but he seemed happy-ish.

At least he was adjusting. That was all we could ask for.

CHAPTER 14

"ALL RIGHT! THIS IS THE WINNING RACE AND WILL determine this year's victor of The Beach Games!" Noah roared through his bullhorn.

Lincoln and I were on the same team with Noah and Shea. We had totally made them do a couples' thing, and we were tied for first place.

I gave Tiffany a side glare. Shea nearly killed Noah for inviting her, but I guess she was considered family because of her stupid parents who I'd never even met. These alleged amazing parents were BFFs of Noah's and Lincoln's parents, so we had to include Tiffany, and to top it all off, the bitch was tied with us for first. She'd brought some brute of a guy to be the final member of her group, a Celestial who'd graduated years ago and must have been pushing thirty.

"Pick one representative to swim the obstacle course!" Noah shouted into the bullhorn.

My eyes flicked to Tiffany, who rolled out her shoulders. "I was first place at the national swim team meet, three years in a row," she cooed. "I'll do it."

Her two lackeys and old Celestial dude nodded.

"I'm doing it!" I shouted to my group.

Lincoln frowned, lowering his voice. "Babe, no offense, but I'm a better swimmer."

I glared at him. "It's Tiffany" was all I said.

He threw his arms up in defeat and Shea grinned. "Okay, now if you have a chance to drown her—"

"Ladies, please. Good vibes," Noah intervened.

Now it was Shea's turn to glare, and Noah stepped back two paces. When would these boys learn not to intervene in our feud?

I nodded to Shea. I obviously wasn't going to drown her, but if she caught an elbow to the eye, oopsie.

Noah got on the bullhorn again. "Okay, racers, take your marks."

Tiffany and I walked up to the line that had been drawn in the sand. Because we were in first and second place, we were the first heat. At the line was Blake with a stopwatch.

"There are obstacles in the water, so in order to win, you need to swim through the four hula hoops, grab the toy seal floaty, and make it back here. Anything goes."

Tiffany zipped up her wetsuit and grinned. "Sounds fun."

I was having trouble getting my bubble butt into my wet suit. Finally, with a little help from Shea, I zipped mine up and stood next to Bitchany.

"Ready, Archie?" she sneered.

'*May you die one hundred deaths,*' Sera cursed at Tiffany from her spot in Shea's hands.

I chuckled and then the whistle blew.

Tiffany took off like her ass was on fire and I scrambled after her, my feet sinking into the sand. The small crowd cheered as Tiffany hit the water and started to kick like a freaking fish. She had perfect form.

I exploded from my place at the edge of the water and dove into the sea. The moment the cold October water hit my face, I had to force myself not to suck in liquid. Tiffany's foot was right in front of my face and I reached out, grabbing it and yanking. Yeah, it was a dirty trick, but Noah said *anything goes*. She was pulled toward me and I crawled over her, making it to the first ring. I swam through the purple glittering hula hoop right before she socked me in the back.

I shouted underwater, releasing all my air, and then came up for a fresh breath. Tiffany was ahead of me now, but my legs were kicking like crazy. I needed that freaking floating seal. I could see it in the water bopping with the surf.

'*Take her down!*' Sera cheered from the shoreline.

I often wondered how far Sera and I could be from one another and still have a mental conversation.

With renewed strength, I burst through the next hoop and caught Tiffany just as she was going through the third one. I repeated the same move, yanking her skinny-ass leg and dragging her behind me, then swam through the third hoop with ease. But that time I was prepared for her back punch, and instead I flipped around underwater, her fist inches away from my back, and kicked out with my foot, connecting with her crotch.

Damn. I'd never kicked a chick in the crotch before. I kinda felt bad, but then again it was Tiffany, so the feeling dissipated quickly. She rose to the surface for air while I gunned it through the fourth hoop, and surfaced to find the seal. He was five feet from me—I so had this!

I paddled like crazy, and when my fingers wrapped around the seal's leg, I cried out in triumph. That triumph was short-lived, however. The moment I spun around to race to the shore with my sweet seal, Tiffany was waiting with a purple glowing spell in her hand.

My first instinct was to duck underwater and avoid getting hit by whatever the spell was, but I'd only made it halfway under when the purple light crashed over my head and my limbs went weak. Tiffany snatched the seal away and blew me a kiss.

"Sorry, Archie."

Rage boiled just underneath the surface of my skin as I slowly paddled to stay above water. Like a drunken thousand-pound seal, I had no grace and no speed. Tiffany took off like a freaking Olympian swimmer while I struggled to even move forward with the spell attacking my body.

My body... An idea struck me then. Noah had said we'd have to swim through the four hoops and get the seal, then get back to shore. He didn't say swim back to shore. I suddenly wondered if Tiffany's spell extended to my wings, which hadn't been out at the time she'd spelled me.

Acting quickly, I unzipped the top portion of my wet suit to expose my back, yelping as cold water rushed in, making my breath hitch. Once the wet suit was at my waist, I snapped my wings out and flapped above the water.

Hell yes.

The crowd on the beach roared.

Tiffany was about twenty feet from the shoreline when she popped up, to get a breath of air, and heard the cheering. She probably thought it was for her. How cute.

When she dipped back under, her hand carrying the seal came up above the waterline, and I swooped down to get it. It was a bit tricky, pivoting my slow-ass body forward to grab it with my fast wings, but when my fingers wrapped around the seal's tail, I yanked as hard as I could.

Tiffany broke the surface, screaming at me, but I didn't stick around to see her wrath. I beelined for the shore, where everyone shouted and clapped there. Lincoln was grinning ear to ear, but not as much as Shea. As I landed on the sand and walked slowly across the finish line, I could already feel the spell on my limbs wearing off.

When Noah announced me as the winner, I spun around to see Tiffany, closely resembling a drowned rat, with an evil look in her eye.

If our feud had died out before, it was alive and well now.

———•———

The next three months passed rather monotonously. Shea and I trained with Noah and Lincoln to win Fight Night, and one weekend a month, we went out into the depressing war zone—though Lincoln seemed to always give me the boring safe things to do like deliver water to an army camp.

Shea and I had awoken to a rat in our room a few weeks ago, but since no one else in the school had a rat problem, we figured it was Tiffany. Now it was Monday and I was in battle class, trying to think of all the ways I could kill her and make it look like an accident.

Shea and I were practicing drills when Noah walked in. She grinned, stepping away from me to greet him, but when we saw his face, my stomach dropped.

Something was wrong.

The normally handsome, wink-happy Lothario was sweating, and he looked like a puppy had died. "I need Brielle and Shea to come with me," Noah told our professor, who nodded curtly.

My best friend and I followed him out of class. When we reached the hallway, he checked to make sure we were alone, then spun around to face us.

"What is it?" Shea reached for him.

"Lincoln's been taken." Those words left his mouth in what seemed like slow motion.

Lincoln. Taken. My brain was refusing to process it. The room swayed a little as my heart hammered in my chest, pumping my body full of adrenaline. Shea reached out for me as I finally found my voice.

"Tell me everything. When? By who? What efforts are we taking to find him?" I was in warrior mode now, pushing all emotion to the side, and being practical. Lincoln had taught me as much. A weeping girlfriend wasn't going to find him.

Noah grimaced. "We were out on patrol in Inferno and the Tainted Army came out of nowhere. Pulled up in a van and called Lincoln by name. The next thing I knew, they threw a smoke spell, and I heard tires screeching. Lincoln was gone. I went airborne to follow the van, but they have some advanced-level magic hiding him."

I was going to be sick. Tainted Army. Those assholes from the Tainted Academy had known Lincoln by name, and it had bothered him. Now they were out there fighting for the demons? Enslaving humans for them? It made me sick.

I started to pace the short hall. "Raphael. Michael. What are they doing?"

"They put a rescue team together an hour ago, but our Light Mages can't find him. Even Claymore is at a loss."

Oh my God. I couldn't do this. A stifled sob left my throat then as my tough girl façade cracked.

Shea put both hands on my shoulders. "We'll find him. If the Dark Mages are hiding him, there must be some other way to track him."

I'd forgotten Sera was with me until she vibrated on my hip.

'I can't find Lincoln, but I can find his sword. If he's still got it with him, we'll find him.'

Hope burst in my chest at her words. "Noah, did Lincoln have his sword on him when they took him?"

Noah's forehead crinkled but he nodded. "Yeah, he had it."

'I can trace another person's infinity weapon so long as I've met that weapon.'

I didn't understand it, but Sera had certainly 'met' Lincoln's weapon hundreds of times.

"Sera can trace his infinity weapon," I told them and started running to the parking lot.

164

"Awesome. I'll tell Michael!" Noah shouted after me, then whipped out his phone.

We made quick work of getting to the parking lot where Darren was at the wheel of his SUV, Blake sitting shotgun. I quickly told them the news, and Noah, Shea, and I squeezed into the back. Then we were off.

The entire drive, I repeated one thing incessantly: *Lincoln's okay, Lincoln's okay*. He had to be okay. I couldn't even conceive of a world where Lincoln was lost or dead. I felt physically ill, my hands shaking from adrenaline.

When we arrived at the base camp within the war zone, we exited the car quickly, making our way to Michael and the twenty-man battalion that stood with him.

"Brielle!" Michael sounded cheery.

Mr. Claymore and Raphael were both with him.

"Is it true? Sera can track Lincoln?" Raphael asked me, pride gleaming in his eyes.

I nodded.

'I just need a bit of archangel blood. Preferably Michael,' Sera told me.

My eyes bugged.

'What! You never told me that!'

'Well how else am I going to find his weapon? I need some powerful blood to work my magic,' she said matter-of-factly, like that made total sense.

Blood magic. My weapon did blood magic.

165

'I'm just supposed to ask one of them for their blood?' I screamed at her, my face pinching in anger.

Michael frowned. "Is something wrong?"

I laughed nervously, and now Raphael was looking at me like I was crazy.

'It has to be one of the archangels who have blessed Lincoln with power, so either will do, really,' Sera said, as if that was helping.

My hand nervously ran through my hair. "Well, I guess Sera needs archangel blood for her magic finder spell… So…"

Oh God, kill me now.

Michael stepped forward, bringing with him the air of power, and held out his arm. "No problem. I trust you, Brielle."

Those blazing blue eyes looked right through me, straight into my soul, and I nearly covered my chest in an attempt to hide. I felt so exposed, so…raw.

Archangel Michael trusted me. Angel blood fetched a fair price on the black market, and he trusted me.

'Come on, Lincoln's being tortured for all we know!' Sera shouted, making me jump a little.

Breaking out of my Michael mesmerization, I pulled Sera out.

'Just a little taste is all I need,' she instructed.

Gross.

Michael held his arm out, and I reluctantly sliced

a little cut on the upper part of his left forearm. He didn't even flinch, but I did.

I just freaking cut Archangel Michael. I was totally going to hell.

'Oh yum. He tastes even better than he smells.'

Oh. My. God. My face fell.

'You're completely nuts,' I told my blade.

She didn't seem to care. *'Get in the car. I've got a beacon on your man.'*

Relief washed over me. "She's got him!"

I ran to the car, Noah hopping in the driver seat while I sat shotgun. The rest of our crew piled in the back, with Michael and his warriors following us in one of the Fallen Army-issued fifteen-passenger vans. They were blacked out, and had such severe tinting you couldn't even see inside of them.

Hopefully we would be low key.

'Go right,' Sera urged suddenly.

"Right!" I shouted, and Noah slammed on the brakes, cutting the wheel to make the turn.

I muttered an apology to him and told Sera to give me more notice next time.

'I can't. Go left,' she shouted.

"Left here!" I pointed to the road we were about to pass.

The tires squealed as we made the turn, and Noah gave me a glare.

"She can't help it! Drive slower," I shouted at him.

"Yeah," Shea backed me up.

Noah sighed, easing on the brakes and slowing to a crawl. We made our way slowly into the city of Inferno, almost to the outer edge where there were high gates and tons of demon guards.

"What's that?" I whispered, staring at the gates.

"We call it the city of Limbo. It's a demon stronghold," Noah explained.

Oh God. If Lincoln was in there, I would cry.

'Left and stop. He's here. The big brick building up ahead,' Sera told me.

I relayed her words to Noah, and we turned left and parked. Up ahead, there was indeed a large red brick industrial building. It felt like the gauntlet all over again.

'How can you see when you don't have eyes?' I asked Sera.

'I'm an angel blade. I don't need eyes to see,' she retorted.

Show-off.

Not one of us dared leave the car for fear of tipping them off and them killing or moving Lincoln.

"I have a plan," Michael said over the radio. "Our Light Mage says this building is heavily guarded, and I don't want to spook them. Brielle, do you feel ready to do a mission?"

To save my boyfriend from Tainted Army assholes? Hell yes!

"Yes sir," I told him. Raphael could be 'Raph,' but Michael was always 'sir.'

"Let's fly, then." And the line went dead.

Noah pivoted toward me. "Are you sure you're ready for this? You can say no."

I rolled my eyes. "Are you kidding? I'm going to help Lincoln."

Noah shrugged. "Lincoln would want me to try to stop you at least once. Now, I can say I did. Good luck. We'll be right behind you once you secure him." He clipped a walkie-talkie to my belt and nodded.

Lincoln would want Noah to protect me, because Lincoln was always protecting me. The thought made my heart pinch.

I'm coming.

Shea reached over and squeezed my bicep, and I squeezed her hand back before exiting the car. Michael was waiting for me on the curb, wearing a hooded sweater. His wings were drawn as far behind him as possible so as to appear normal to a passerby, I assumed.

The moment I stepped in beside him, he started to walk.

"We'll land on the roof. They won't expect that. When we get inside, I'll fight you a path to Lincoln. I suspect he's restrained, so untether him and call for backup."

I nodded. Didn't sound too hard.

Michael grabbed my arm. "If at any time you feel your life is in mortal danger, you break a window and fly out of it, understood?"

No way.

"Yes, sir."

He grinned in a mischievous way that told me he most definitely had read my mind.

Just then, his wings snapped out and he blasted off the concrete into the sky. I stared at his miraculous flight in awe.

'Get up there, you dingbat!' Sera shouted.

Oh shit. Right.

My wings snapped out, and then I was right behind him, flapping and pumping my black wings to crawl high above Inferno. It was a ghastly town, full of demons, poverty, and death. I wanted to free the humans being held there. Knowing that was ultimately the Fallen Army's plan, I couldn't wait to be a part of that.

The air was freezing, as we were super high. Higher than I normally went in practice drills with Lincoln.

Michael suddenly pivoted in the sky and started to drop down, me right on his tail. Lincoln Grey was not someone I planned on ever living without.

Our boots landed on the rooftop, and Michael wasted no time cutting down the Monkshood demon that stood guard. His sword *literally* cut through the demon like he was made of butter, leaving a blue fire in its wake. It was both a glorious and disgusting sight to behold.

Next, Michael used his sword to cut the door

handle off, again like butter. I was starting to see why the demons would find his sword so valuable.

He peered inside the now-open doorway and lurched backward just in time to miss having his face marred with acid.

God, the Snakeroot demons were populating like crazy! Michael sliced him down too, while I just stood there stupidly, holding Sera, waiting to see if he would need any help.

He didn't.

We ran down the stairs two by two until we reached a closed door.

Cut off handle, kill demons guarding, rinse and repeat.

We'd gone down three levels when I heard it—Lincoln's strangled cry one floor below.

"Lincoln!" I shouted, my entire body clenching as my fight or flight mode kicked in. Pivoting, I beelined for the doorway, leaving Michael to fight the Yew demon on the current floor we were on alone. I ran full speed down the stairs to the floor below, just in time to see two big-ass Tainted Academy students dragging a barely conscious Lincoln out the door. His feet, legs, and wings were bound with thick leather-looking straps.

How. Dare. They.

Anger exploded inside of me as I thrust Sera in front of me and released a savage battle cry. She pulsed a white light so bright that the men holding

Lincoln were forced to drop him and cover their eyes. I lunged forward, slicing into the brute nearest me and gouging his side, letting my knife sink into his rib cage.

You kidnap my boyfriend, I cut you.

He fell to the ground with a groan, and then I was working on the next guy. He was still momentarily blinded, which was nice, but he also looked like a Dark Mage. Slashing out, I carved an X into his outstretched arm.

While he was distracted, I pulled out my walkie-talkie. "I've got Lincoln. Send backup."

I'd just replaced the walkie when I saw an angry reddish magical ball hurtling toward my face. Arching my back so it wouldn't collide with me, I dodged it, but also fell to the ground in the process.

That's when I saw Michael casually watching my little fight from the stairs. How long had he been standing there?

"Why don't you get Lincoln out? I'll finish up here." He winked.

Whoa. His wink was powerful, doing things to my insides. A sexy angel wink was like two Lincoln winks.

I simply nodded from my place on the ground, and then Michael was leaping over me to take on the Tainted Academy asshole.

"Brielle," Lincoln croaked.

I shot up into a standing position and started to

cut off his wing bindings first, then sliced his ankle restraints, and finally the ones around his hands. All within a minute, thanks to Sera's help.

Grabbing Lincoln's right arm, I pulled it over my head so he could lean on me, and we started to walk down the steps to the bottom floor.

"I can't believe Noah let you come," Lincoln growled in anger.

"It's great to see you too." I rolled my eyes. "I'm glad you're alive," I added curtly. He was limping; they'd clearly injured him.

He sighed and then stopped, turning to face me in the darkened stairwell. "Thanks for coming, I'm happy to see you," he amended.

That was better.

I heard footsteps coming up the stairs and held Sera before me, ready to blind whoever it was, but when Noah's head peeked over the railing, I relaxed.

"Upstairs." I pointed to where Michael was.

Noah took the stairs two at a time, only stopping to pat his best friend's shoulder for a moment. When we finally made it outside and were walking to a worried-looking Shea, who was keeping the car warm, I asked Lincoln what was on my mind.

"What did Tainted Academy want?"

Lincoln growled. "Maybe just a personal vendetta for coming on campus that day, but the guy knew everything about me, so I think it goes deeper."

Bastards.

From now on, I was keeping an eye on Lincoln, just as he did for me. It looked like I wasn't the only one in danger.

CHAPTER 15

TWO WEEKS AFTER LINCOLN'S KIDNAPPING, HE had fully healed and was barking orders as usual.

"The big fight is next weekend!" Lincoln told Shea and me at our weekly training. "So I want to change it up a bit. Do something more realistic," he declared.

I raised one eyebrow at Shea. We'd been training like machines every spare chance we had; I wasn't sure 'changing it up' would teach us anything new.

Just then, the double doors opened, Tiffany and one of her sheep walked in—Tiffany #2.

"You're early. I haven't told them yet," Lincoln groaned to the blonde Light Mage.

"Um, what?" I pinned my boyfriend with a death

glare. If he thought I was fighting Tiffany, he was so sorely mistaken. I would kill her and then go to jail, and it would be bad.

"No, no." Shea raised her hands. "Bad idea. We'll all kill each other."

Lincoln motioned for the Tiffanys to come closer. "I know an active feud exists between you guys, so it's the best way to test your fighting ability. The hits will be real. You'll have a week to heal before the real fight, and Mr. Claymore has made a spelled drink that will keep you from doing any serious damage—no severed limbs or deaths. I tried it out myself last night on Noah."

Noah waved from the back of the room, and when Shea looked at him, he winked.

"And why would I help Archie train for her little death match?" Tiffany droned, crossing her arms.

Lincoln grinned like he had an animal caught in a trap. "Because you've dreamed about punching her in the face since the day she got here. Now's your only chance."

She smirked. "True. All right, I'm in."

I raised my hand and Lincoln called on me.

"Just one question. Will Mr. Claymore's spell keep me from ripping out her hair?" I pulled Sera and dropped into my fighting stance.

Shea snorted, trying to conceal a laugh, but Tiffany squared off with me, fire gleaming in her eyes.

Oh yeah. I'd dreamed of this day for almost two years now. Shit was going to go down.

"Whoa, whoa. Let's talk rules," Lincoln pleaded.

"Screw the rules. Give us the drink," Tiffany spat.

Lincoln looked to me and I nodded. I was going to chug that drink and then try to rip off her head.

"Damn, I'm totally videotaping this," Noah chuckled from the corner of the training room.

I pointed Sera at him and she shot a small pulse of light out, making him shriek and drop his phone.

"No way," I roared.

He groaned and threw his hands up. "Okay, okay."

Lincoln handed me a shot glass brimming with a deep purple fluid. Without a word, I tipped it back and chugged.

Oh good Lord, that was nasty. Like black licorice and gritty sand.

Tiffany did the same, then Shea and Tiffany #2.

"All right, in the—"

I cut Lincoln off with a battle cry.

Bitch was going down.

I slashed my dagger out wildly, catching Tiffany's arm and drawing blood.

"*That* was for Luke," I told her.

She looked down at her bleeding arm in shock, but I wasted no time attacking again. This was going to be epic.

My leg came up and I socked her in the chest

177

with my boot, knocking her backward. Her blonde ponytail dramatically bobbed as she went down. "*That* was for calling me Archie!" I exclaimed.

Shea was already in her own fight with Tiffany's clone, so I kept my focus solely on the queen bitch herself.

She was two seconds from getting her hair ripped out. As I dropped to my knees to straddle the evil Light Mage, her hands came up and a purple ball of fire slammed into my chest, hurling me into the air and then dropping me. I came down hard, jamming my right ankle and flopping ungracefully to my side.

Still, I grinned. "Now there's the Bitchany I know."

Lincoln and Noah were watching with what looked like a mixture of horror and fascination as my wings popped out and I tore across the room. Tiffany crouched, ready for me, but even with her sword up, she wasn't ready for this. Sera shot out with a blinding white light, and Tiffany dropped her sword to cover her eyes. Then I slammed into her with the force of a bullet, grabbing her by the throat and dragging her across the floor until she crashed into the far wall. I held her there by the throat, knowing I had her. Lincoln would call it off, and I would be the victor.

Suddenly, she latched onto my steel arm cuffs with both hands and they started to heat up, like *really* hot, really fast.

"Lincoln's parents and my parents always wanted us to end up together. Once he's done slumming it, he'll settle down with a proper girl like me. You're just the interim chick," she spat.

Holy shit, my skin was smoking. *Literally*.

I tore my right hand away from her and flattened my palm before driving it into her nose. The impact with her cartilage sent warm crimson fluid spurting over my hand at the same time a popping noise sounded in her nose.

She let my cuffs go and I released her neck, and then we were falling.

"All right, that's enough!" Lincoln shouted.

My cuffs were still hot as hell, so I clawed at the edges and ripped them off, letting them drop to the floor.

"Noah!" Tiffany shrieked behind me. "She broke my nose!"

Noah sauntered over slowly. "I see that. Bummer."

Tiffany glared at him with murder in her eyes. "You better be able to put it back the way it was."

Shea and Tiffany #2 looked bruised and bloodied, but nothing too bad.

My boyfriend was trying to contain his smirk. "Thank you, Tiffany, for agreeing to this exercise."

She gave him a sugary smile, dripping with malice. "I hope your girlfriend loses and stays in Demon City where she belongs." Then she spun on her heel and left the room. But not before shouting Noah's name to follow.

Once we were alone, I sighed. "Oh man, that felt good!"

Shea limped over to me. "Please tell me you ripped a little chunk of her hair out."

"Okay, okay, enough evil plotting. That was really great. It gave me a sense of what to expect for Fight Night, but..." Lincoln turned on me. "You held back. She's your archnemesis, and yet you held back."

I frowned. "What do you mean?" Did he expect me to produce the dark energy whip and cut her head off? Because that could definitely be arranged.

He tapped my necklace. "Your Light Magic. I was hoping to get a good show. Maybe even see an orb."

Yeah, my Light Magic. Whoops.

I hadn't actually used it since I'd returned from Hell with Sera. I technically wasn't sure it still worked, and Mr. Rincor agreed that we shouldn't really mess with it too much after what happened. So we'd been working on other things, things Sera could do with light and commands I could give her to help my fighting. Ever since I'd taken the necklace off and gone into that dark place...well, it felt like maybe what Noah had said was true. Like maybe my darkness was scared of getting pushed back again, so it rose to the surface and fought for space or whatever.

"Oh yeah." I didn't know what to say. "I didn't want to make an orb and crash for the next few days." That was true, as it did knock out my energy. He knew that from last time, so maybe I could just play that up and he'd be none the wiser.

Lincoln looked skeptically at me. "But you still feel it, right? Your light magic?"

What was normal for Lincoln wasn't normal for me. I was sure he could just close his eyes and 'feel' his light magic, but I couldn't really. I didn't work like that. I'd been given both light and dark magic, and that was my normal. But he wouldn't understand that.

"Yep." I gave him a cheery smile.

"So," Shea interjected, "I know my ex-boss. He'll go back on his word the second he can. I think we should have a blood contract written up so we both agree to the terms of your mom's release. Otherwise, we might just be giving him a million dollars, with him telling us to screw off."

Lincoln nodded. "I was thinking the same thing, and I've spoken to Raph and Mr. Claymore about it. They have agreed to draft one up. Blood contracts are magically binding, so they take a lot of work."

Damn. I was glad they were on the ball, because if it was just me in charge, I'd probably get myself screwed over.

"Okay," I told them both. "Just let me know if you need my blood or whatever."

Lincoln swallowed hard and nodded. When he did that, it was like a nervous tic. The hard swallow, his Adam's apple bobbing—all signs he was hiding something.

"Out with it! What are you hiding?" I put a hand on my sore hip.

He groaned. "You know me too well. That's not fair."

I did the time in this relationship, and now I knew him well enough to catch him in lies. Perfectly fair.

He sighed. "I won't be needing your blood. I'm the one signing the contract. If it all goes wrong, I want the fallout to be on me, not you girls."

I clenched my jaw. "No way!"

Lincoln nodded. "Yes way. I looked at the rules last night. Fights end in either death or submission. If you girls submit, you walk away with your life, and what does Grim get for letting you fight? He'll want some type of collateral. They always do. So I'm the collateral."

Shea was staring at him with her mouth open, as was I.

"If we lose, we'll give him Sera." I hated it the moment the words left my mouth, but Lincoln wasn't something I could afford to lose, and I had faith I would win.

'I *understand*,' Sera said in a melancholy tone. She was part of me, and she loved Lincoln too.

Lincoln reached out and put a hand on my shoulder. That was his let-down pose; he was about to let me down, and the hand on shoulder was my consolation prize.

"I suggested that, but the archangels agreed that a seraph blade should never be allowed in the hands of the demons."

I mean, I loved Sera, and I knew she was powerful but...she was just a weapon.

'Hey,' she retorted.

'Sorry.'

Lincoln leaned close to whisper in my ear. "I overheard Michael saying Sera could open the gates of Heaven. She has that much power. Can you imagine if the demons had the key to Heaven?"

My whole body went rigid, and chills broke out on my arms.

"Secrets don't make friends," Shea pouted from a few feet away, but I was still spinning his words in my head.

'Is that true? Can you open the gates of Heaven?' I asked my infinity weapon.

'How should I know? I've been stuck in a cabinet for over a decade waiting for you, with little memory of before that. But it feels right,' she told me.

Wow. I didn't even know what to say to that.

"Okay, well, we're going to win, so..." We had to win now. There was no way I could let Lincoln work off my mom's debt.

He leaned down and kissed my forehead. "I have faith in you."

For some reason, those words made me feel worse. Lincoln was putting his life in my hands, and I wasn't sure that was such a good idea.

CHAPTER 16

"I FEEL SICK," SHEA SAID AS SHE PACED LINCOLN'S carpet.

"Me too," I admitted.

Chloe, Luke, Lincoln, and Noah were all sitting around, waiting with us until it was time to leave for Fight Night.

Lincoln stood. "You've trained, we've gotten Grim to agree to the contract, and your mother is on board with the plan. You got this."

Hearing his logical words should have made me feel better, but it didn't. This wasn't Angel City we were going to, it was Demon City. Home of the rule breakers, risk takers, and stab you in the backers. They weren't going to play by the rules. We had to be ready for every dirty trick in the book.

Shea pulled a baggie out of her pocket. "Magic is allowed. I made these energy lozenges. As we weaken with each fight, we'll take one and get an adrenaline surge. It'll carry us through to the end. Hopefully."

I nodded. The lozenges would be much needed in the end I was sure.

Chloe cleared her throat. "How many fights are there?"

Chloe's dad, owner of the Third Eye Moon club and basically vampire overlord, was sending some of his men to the fight to make sure Grim kept his word if we won.

"Seven." Noah stood. "Lincoln and I won't make it through all of them, so we're going to go in shifts. Lincoln will go for the first four fights. I'll go for the last three. You're allowed to get healings, so we'll both be healing you between the fights."

It was a good plan. I had Sera, and we'd been training like crazy. At this point, Shea and I could join some elite supernatural assassin force if there were one. We were killing machine badasses, but I still felt a lump in my throat.

"Yeah," I answered absentmindedly.

"And Chloe and Luke will be able to be there the whole time because..." He rubbed the back of his neck.

"Because we're demon gifted, born of the demons' loins." Chloe smirked at Noah.

Lincoln was watching me, assessing, and sizing me up with those ocean-blue eyes.

"Can I speak to you privately for a minute?" my boyfriend asked me, nodding toward his room.

My stomach became a ball of nerves, as I started to walk in that direction. Once he'd closed the door behind him, he snapped around to face me.

"Stop that!" he hissed.

My eyes widened. "Stop what?"

His shirt was so tight I could see the bulging muscles just underneath. Lincoln was a warrior through and through. He crossed the space between us, cradling my face.

"Stop doubting yourself. What the hell is there to be nervous about? You've got this," he declared.

My body melted at his touch, my nerves chased away by his words.

"How many other kids there do you think have had round-the-clock training from some of the best military officers in the field?" he asked.

I grinned. "Isn't Noah supposed to be the cocky one?"

He chuckled. "Just think about it. They'll be scrappy, dirty, but you and Shea are well-trained, precise, and you're both very, very powerful."

He was right. Shea and I were born scrappy, but we'd also learned how to be diligent and purposeful in our attacks. We'd also been field-trained in the Fallen Army on our weekends out. We were ready.

I'm getting my mom back. Tonight.

Lincoln brushed his thumb along my lower lip. "Do you honestly think I'd let you sign up for something I didn't believe you could do?"

I shook my head. "No."

His lips tugged into a radiant smile. "Then you need to believe in yourself. All the big athletes say half the game is played and won in their heads. No more negative thoughts, okay?"

I smirked. "I'm usually the positive one."

He leaned in and dropped a kiss on my neck. "Well, I'm happy to be of service."

I moaned. Speaking of service, I could think of something that needed a little servicing to get the tension out. It was so nice now that Lincoln had his own big apartment. No more rocking the trailer.

My eyes snapped open and I pushed him back as a thought struck me. "Oh my God! My mom has nowhere to live! If I bring her back, she'll need a place until she can get on her feet. Is your trailer still available? Do you think...?" I felt bad for even asking, but I had no other options.

Lincoln looked down at me with a knowing gaze. "I'm surprised it took you this long to think about it."

I raised one eyebrow in confusion. "Is that a yes?"

He shook his head. "I'm not making the mother of the woman I love live in my old tiny trailer. Besides, if she's as good a cook as you say she is, I'll enjoy all the meals."

My throat cinched with emotion. "What are you saying?"

He trailed a finger down my cheek. "I'm saying a few days ago, Noah helped me set up the guest room. It has a bed and dresser now."

I had to bite my tongue to keep from sobbing. "That's your music room."

He shrugged. "I'll turn it into a music room when she's gone."

"Lincoln." The tears started falling. He was a twenty-four-year-old guy who hated demon slaves, and yet was willing to live with my mom who was one. "You want to live with my mom? Are you sure? She can be annoying," I warned him.

He laughed, but then a dark look crossed his face. "I'd give anything to have my mom back to annoy me for just one day."

I swallowed hard. "I didn't mean that. I—"

He waved it off. "I know. I'm just saying it'll be nice. I'm looking forward to it."

Oh my God. Lincoln Grey was taking my mom into his apartment.

Marry me now and have my babies.

"Is she all packed?" he inquired.

I nodded. My mom had freaked about the fight at first, but then I'd told her about my dark magic whip and strangling necktie and she'd come around to the idea. "She's just waiting for us to stop by after." I was totally doing the positive thing.

189

"Ready?"

I nodded. "Those bitches are going down."

———·———

After Noah said goodbye to Shea with a disgusting make-out session against the wall outside Lincoln's apartment, we hit the road. Luke's aunt lived in Demon City and was a demon slave, so he'd gotten two passes permitting him to visit her for a few hours for him and Chloe. Shea and I were of course permitted as fighters, and Lincoln and Noah had our two guest passes. I tried to tamp down the nerves that were making me feel lightheaded with adrenaline.

'You have no idea how psycho I can go if I need to,' Sera told me.

I couldn't help it as I burst out laughing in the car, which earned me a lot of stares.

'I love you, Sera. I have no idea how you got your personality, but I wouldn't change it for the world.'

'I'm just stating the facts. I won't let us lose. Mom is coming home tonight.'

Mom. Just like that, Sera became my sister.

"Hey there, bud, how you doing?" Shea whispered to her circular blades. Then she put her ear up to them and laughed uncontrollably. "Oh stop it, you're so funny!"

I groaned and reached back, smacking her knee.

"Shut up. Don't be jealous," I scolded her.

Shea grinned. "Right, I'm so jealous that you look like a lunatic half the time, talking to your knife."

I knew she was messing with me, and it got me to smile. "Yeah, well, my lunatic ass is going to save you from getting killed tonight." Sera pulsed her light a few times for good measure.

Shea chuckled.

"We're here," Lincoln announced, and holy shit, he was right. We were pulling down the alley that led to Tainted Academy. There were cars all over the place, even pulled up on the sidewalk, and people were walking in big groups to the gates.

There were demons *everywhere*.

Lincoln winced, his breath hitching as we pulled up to the gate.

"You okay?" I reached out to touch his arm.

He nodded. "So many demons in such a small area. It...hurts. But I'll be fine."

The guards at the gate were different this time. They just glanced at our fighter cards and waved us through.

"Special parking in front," the guard barked, then smacked the side of the car door.

Lincoln drove to the front lot, where there was indeed special parking for the participants. So special, in fact, that the spots were reserved with our names on them. Our sign read: "Fallen Academy douchebags."

"I hate this place," Shea growled.

"Me too. We're almost out of here. For good," I told her.

We wasted no time, parking and rushing through the crowds to get inside. I wanted time to warm up, learn all the rules, and scope the competitors.

After signing in, we were told to go in the back to the competitors' lounge, and that we'd have to leave our friends.

The auditorium was packed. There was a circular cage in the middle about twenty feet in diameter, with people crammed around it as far as the eye could see. Secondary seating was up in the bleachers on a second level.

Lincoln grasped my hand. "You got this," he murmured and kissed me, his lips lingering just long enough to let me know he was worried that I might not have this.

"I'll be fine," I told him.

He nodded. "If not, have Shea create a portal back to school and jump through it. I'll get Chloe and Luke out."

And there it was. I knew he'd have a backup plan just in case. But if I did that, my mom was as good as gone. Grim would be livid, and there'd be more of a hunt for me than there already was.

I just nodded.

After giving Chloe and Luke a quick hug, Shea and I made our way to the back room. Two guards stood before it, requesting our IDs, and then we were in.

The moment we stepped into the crowded room, all eyes turned and silence descended upon the crowd. I recognized a few faces, and it was like a punch to the gut. I was going to have to fight some of my old friends.

"Shea, dear, we've missed you," a girl with green hair cooed.

"Fuck off," Shea spat and pulled out her blades.

Whoa. Shea was ready to throw down. That was good, but we needed to not get jumped before our first match.

I placed a hand on Shea's arm, pulling her to the corner of the room where I saw two familiar faces— Ben and Stephanie. I hadn't seen them since the Awakening, but I was hoping I could still count them as allies. At least until the fighting started.

They looked up at us and gave a half smile. My eyes flicked to the insignia on their stark white jumpsuits. Steph was a Necro like my mom, and Ben was a Nightblood.

"Hey," Stephanie whispered, then walked a bit farther away until we were at the back of the room, leaning against the exit door.

"Can't really be seen making friends with you guys," she murmured, looking out onto the crowd.

Oh damn.

"I get it." I leaned against the door and started to scan the crowd.

Not gonna lie, everyone looked freaking vicious.

They were tatted up, weaponed up, and wore psychotic murderer expressions.

Stephanie's lips didn't move, but I still heard her voice in a low whisper. "They've got plans for you girls. There's no way they'll let Fallen Academy students win."

Shea raised one eyebrow. "What kind of plans?"

Stephanie shrugged, looking casually out onto the crowd of kids who were starting to run warm-up drills, and seemed to have lost interest in us—for the time being. "Just shady shit, like extra stashed weapons and spells the teachers made."

Freaking fabulous.

"Well, we're winning. We're doing this to get my mom out," I explained to her.

For the first time, she faced me. I could see Tainted Academy had been hard on her. Her once-perfect nose looked like it'd been broken multiple times, and the red crescent moon tattoo on her forehead was a reminder of what she was, and what she would always be.

"I heard. My cousin lives in your mom's building. If we go up against each other, we'll make it look real, but we'll submit," she told me.

Ben, who stood tall next to her, nodded his agreement. "If it gets someone out of this hellhole, then I'm down. You guys have always been cool," he stated.

Emotion tightened my throat. I hadn't been

expecting that. "Thanks, guys." I wanted to hug them, cry, show how much their words meant to me, but I couldn't. Not there.

She gave a weak smile. "We should go work the room. See ya."

With her out of sight, I stared at Shea. "Okay, that was seriously cool of them. I was—"

The door popped open behind me, and a firm grip landed on my arm, pulling me backward out of the room, and into a dark hallway.

I went to scream, but a hand clamped around my mouth.

Shea burst into the dark hallway after me, purple magic ready, but when she saw who held me she stopped. "James?"

The hand fell away from my mouth. "Go back inside, Shea. I just need to talk to Brielle alone for a minute, and no one can know I did," he whispered.

Shea looked at him for another second and I nodded. "It's okay," I told her.

Reluctantly, my bestie slipped back into the room.

Once the door closed behind her, I spun around.

I'd known James would be declared a Sighted at his Awakening, but seeing him wearing the white Tainted Academy uniform with the purple third eye emblem on his chest still shocked me. Almost two years at Fallen Academy and I hadn't met one. They did special classes and were kept away from the students because it was too much energy or something. Not to mention they were extremely rare and prized individuals.

"James," I breathed.

He stared at his hands. "My gift is a curse."

Frowning, I stepped closer. "What? Are you okay?"

He swallowed hard. "Yes. But you aren't. You won't be."

My stomach dropped.

"Am I going to lose tonight?" I really had thought I'd win this fight, and come back with my mom. If he told me otherwise, I would be devastated.

He waved his hand. "I'm not talking about tonight. Brielle, Lucifer wants you."

That statement sent chills crawling up my back and down my arms.

"I know." I peeled open my shirt and showed him my chest tattoo.

He shook his head. "No. You know the vision every Sighted at Fallen Academy gets, that you'll go into the underworld and kill him? It's not the *only* vision."

My eyes widened. *He knows about that?* "What do you mean?"

James sighed. "Every Sighted here sees something different. I... I saw you training with him. Becoming like him. Living down there with him." He pointed to the ground, to Hell.

Bile rose in my throat.

No.

"I would never do that!" I whisper-screamed.

He looked sad. "I've seen it. He trains you. You... create demons with him. Down there."

I was going to throw up. It was absolute lies. I crossed my arms. "James, there's no freaking way. Your vision is wrong!"

He shrugged. "I just wanted to warn you. There is another side, another vision, and that's the one Lucifer believes in."

I softened, knowing he was only trying to help. "Thank you. You're a good friend."

He looked off into the distance. "Either way, you'll change the world, Bri. I just haven't decided if for better or worse."

Not what I wanted to hear. That sick feeling was back.

Then he turned and started to walk away.

"Wait! Will I get my mom out of here tonight?"

I mean, after dropping all that shit on me, the least he could do would be to give me some good news.

"If I tell you, it changes the future," he called back. Turning to face me, he glanced at my necklace, the one that pushed the darkness back so I could use my light gifts. "Take the necklace off for tonight. It'll only hinder you."

Then he was gone.

Mother eff.

I felt a panic attack at the edges of my mind. Me training with Lucifer and living in Hell? Was James completely mad? I would *never* do that. There was no situation I could think of that would ever make that happen. Not even with a gun to my head.

The door popped open then and Shea urged me inside.

"We've been paired for our first fight," she told me, slightly paler than her usual color.

I'd have to push this to the back of my mind—*way* back—and focus on my mom and Mikey. She was all we had left, and I was bringing her home tonight.

I unclasped my necklace and slipped it into my pocket, earning me a raised eyebrow from Shea.

"If they're going to fight dirty, so are we," I exclaimed.

Besides, I was pretty sure the necklace didn't really work anyway. Not like it did before I went into Hell to get Sera.

CHAPTER 17

THEY'D ALSO ASSIGNED US THE BIG FENCED-IN ring for our fight, while others were stationed at various taped-off areas outside on the field. The first few fights were just to whittle the numbers down, take out the weak.

As we made our way out to the main ring, the booing started. Shea flipped them off, and they started to roar in excitement. Demon City loved people who were pissed off.

My eyes flicked to the upper corners of the room, to where there were cameras stationed in the eaves. This was totally televised, and even though I'd told her not to, I knew my mother would watch.

"Oh good. This dude grabbed my ass the first day of school, and that chick pinned me down when I got my death mark. They're both dead," Shea informed me through gritted teeth, pointing to our new fighters. The guy was a mountain of a man and clearly over the age limit of twenty-one. He had a full-on beard and smelled of a Beast Shifter. The chick was totally a Dark Mage; looking into her glassy black eyes made my skin crawl. Of course they'd paired us with one of the strongest teams for our first fight. Trying to take us out or injure us in the very beginning seemed to be their plan.

The crowd roared as the gates to the cage opened and the two fighters made their way in.

I saw Lincoln, Chloe, and Luke just off to the side, smooshed into the front row.

My hand caught Shea's arm. "If it gets life threatening, you make a portal back to the academy, okay?" I told her.

She rolled her eyes. "We're not leaving here without Mom."

She'd said it again. Not "your mom," but "*Mom.*" That meant *our* mom. Everything within me welled up at our shared love for that woman.

"I love you, Shea." I tried not to let my voice catch.

"Stop it." She punched my arm lightly. "We got this."

A laugh escaped my throat but quickly died down when I caught sight of Grim. The demon was standing near the open cage gates, glaring at us.

I figured he'd be there, but why did he look like he wanted to talk to me? He'd signed the deal in blood; there was no way he could go back.

When we reached him, and his sulfuric scent, he leaned in. "I found a buyer for your mom and the clinic. Five hundred grand. If you don't win tonight, I sell her."

If that didn't add fuel to the fire, I didn't know what would.

"We're going to win. You're going to get your prize money, and we're taking my mom," I spat, then blasted past him and into the cage.

"Alllllllll right, Demon City!" an announcer roared. "We have a special treat tonight. Two students from Fallen Academy think they're better than our fighters!"

The crowd booed, except for three distinct cheers. Lincoln, Chloe, and Luke were going to get jumped by the crowd if they didn't shut up, but I couldn't focus on them right now.

I let my black wings pop out then and the booing stopped, turning into complete silence marked with a few gasps.

Take that, you judgy bastards.

"Shall we see what these two princesses have for us?" the announcers asked, and the crowd went wild.

An older man, an Abrus demon with gray streaks in his hair, stepped into the cage and met our eyes, looking briefly at my tattoo. He had an evil air about him, above and beyond that of the searing yellow eyes and red felt horns protruding from his forehead. When his eyes met mine, gooseflesh broke out on my arms. "Place your weapons on the floor in the middle of the cage," he instructed.

"What?" My head snapped back. What kind of freaking rule was that?

The Abrus demon grinned, showcasing pointy teeth. "We heard you had a seraph blade. Let's see what it can do. First come, first serve. If you reach the weapons first, you get to pick whichever one you want."

The Dark Mage chick grinned, eyeing Sera on my thigh.

'Let her try. I'll burn her hand off and blind her!' Sera spat.

I tried to keep from smiling as I pulled Sera from the holster, placing her in the center of the room. It felt absolutely awful to be without her, but I knew she could handle herself. If they wanted to play by those rules, I would beat them by those rules.

With a grunt, Shea did the same, leaving her two discs on the floor.

We both backed up to the far wall, weapon-less. The other fighters placed their weapons on the ground as well, a large serrated sword and a spiky mace at the end of a chain.

The Abrus demon held his hands against the cage, and the metal began to light up an electric blue.

"When I leave, this cage will be electrified. The only way out is if you kill your opponent or they submit. If one teammate submits, the entire team is disqualified. No other rules exist," he said with a grin, his blazing yellow eyes gazing over my tattooed chest and black wings with lust.

Freaking creeper.

"Let's get this night started! Last team left standing, gets ooooone miiiiiillion dollars!" the announcer roared.

Just like that, the Abrus demon was gone and a buzzer went off. I scrambled to get my footing, totally unprepared for the start, and ran toward our weapons. The Dark Mage threw something right at me, a purplish black blob spinning through the air, but Shea's own spell collided with it.

I ducked down low, two feet from reaching Sera, when that damn Beast Shifter pulled a switchblade on me. Out of my peripheral vision, I saw the moment he yanked the hidden weapon from behind him. He chucked it, and I reared back in an attempt to dodge the blade, but it sank into my bicep before I even had a chance to get out of the way. Pain exploded in my arm, but I ignored it and reached over with my good hand to pull the knife out swiftly. Lincoln would say there was no time for pain.

Blood started bubbling up out of the wound. I quickly yanked at a strip of cloth I'd knotted around my thigh just for that purpose, tying it off with my teeth while my bestie kept the Dark Mage engaged and I held my eyes on the Beast Shifter. He'd grabbed Sera *and* his sword, and was gunning it for me.

Good luck, asshole.

Just as I thought it, Sera lit up in his hand and he yelped, dropping her.

I was ready.

Bursting forward, I scrambled to pick up my weapon, flinching when the torn muscle in my upper arm protested. As I neared the shifter, I smelled the burning flesh where Sera had scorched him. Using my advantage, I flapped my wings to propel me forward, taking up nearly the entire span of the cage as I hurled myself at him. He tried to hinder my advance with his sword, but I threw my steel cuff up to block him as Sera shot out with a precise beam of light that blinded him.

He let out an animal's roar and started to swipe out blindly. I crouched to the ground, slashing out at his ankles until he went down—Lincoln had taught me all about the Achilles tendon and how vital it was for standing. I was just about to straddle him and hopefully get him to submit when I heard Lincoln's scream, and a second later something slammed into my back. My whole body instantly felt like it was on fire.

A panicked cry ripped from me, and immediately Sera started pulsing power into my hand, traveling up my arm and throughout my body.

'*I can take the fire spell, but then you'll need to drop me because I'll be too hot to hold for at least an hour until I can dispel it,*' she informed me quickly.

I was on fire. I didn't see flames, but it sure as hell felt like it. Sweat poured down my face as my skin reddened, and my hands started to shake.

'*Do it,*' I told her.

The power she'd sent throughout my body then snapped back and instantly sucked the spell out. Suddenly her handle was a searing-hot iron. My hand sprang open and Sera fell to the floor, a red-hot glowing dagger.

I spun on the Dark Mage. Lincoln had prepared me for this, saying for the entire year that I had to learn to fight without Sera. He'd turned my body into a weapon, and I was about to throw down on this bitch.

The Beast Shifter was still moaning, backed against the cage, as far as he could go without touching, slashing out with his sword blindly. My guess was that he was sightless for the next few hours until his healing could kick in.

My gaze went to the floor where Shea had been deposited seconds before. Her ear was bleeding and looked half torn off, but otherwise she looked okay. So why wasn't she getting up?

"Necktie!" Shea shouted, her voice warbled. She must have been under some kind of spell.

Another purple ball flew my way and I fell backward, letting my wings keep me from falling all the way back as I dodged the spell.

Necktie. Shea had said necktie. I hadn't wanted to use my dark magic. Not here, not ever. Lincoln would be disappointed in me.

'Lincoln will only be mad if you die,' Sera stated from her place smoldering on the floor.

She was right, and this Dark Mage had held down my best friend and forced her to take the death mark.

I felt that shadowy power within me rise, and it scared me how quickly and easily it went from being just under the surface of my skin to burning in my throat and begging to come out. I roared and the black inky magic shot from my mouth, slamming into the Dark Mage's neck.

The entire crowd went silent, then gasped, followed by a roar of approval.

"Ladies and gentlemen, Fallen Academy has been holding out on us!" the announcer thundered.

The Dark Mage fell to her knees, clutching her throat as her face turned blue.

"Submit!" I shouted at her.

Could I even call it off if she did? I didn't think I had that much control over it, but I wasn't ready to become a killer tonight.

Her lips barely moved, but she managed to croak the words out. "I...submit."

A buzzer sounded overhead, and the cage door

suddenly sprang open. The metal walls were no longer an electrifying blue.

"The winners of this round are Brielle and Shea from Fallen Academy!" the announcer's voice boomed over the speakers. The crowd went wild with a mixture of cheers and boos.

I held out my hand and tried to call the blackness back from her throat, but it didn't move.

Oh shit.

The girl's eyes were rolling in her head now, and the crowd was starting to shout in panicked screams.

The silver-haired Abrus demon from before burst into the cage and snapped his fingers. The inky black rope fell away from the girl's neck, and she took in a huge gulp of air. My heart was hammering in my chest, the adrenaline pumping into my veins making me feel dizzy.

The Abrus demon looked my way and smiled, stepping closer to me. "Keep up the good work. The Dark Prince is very pleased," he murmured and then walked out, leaving me to realize what I'd done.

I was using all my dark gifts, Lucifer's gifts. Yet I was blessed by four archangels and was not relying on any of my light magic. I'd given too much attention to the darkness, and I could feel it gaining power within me.

Another thing I'd just realized—the Prince of Darkness must have been watching me.

Chills broke out on my arms.

"Brielle!" Lincoln called, standing on the outside of the cage, peering in.

I pulled off my steel arm cuff and ran forward, scooping Sera into it, careful not to touch her because she was still too hot. I was hoping she'd be usable for the next fight, but at that point, I wasn't so sure.

"You okay?" I reached out to my bestie who was sitting down, panting.

Our competitors had been helped out of the cage, and now Lincoln was arguing with the guard at the door to be allowed to help us.

"They can make it out okay," the guard retorted.

"Step aside or I'll take off your head!" Lincoln roared.

Shea wasn't moving to take my offered arm. Something was wrong.

"I...need...my spell lozenge," she panted.

While Lincoln was arguing with the guard, Chloe zipped through the open cage using her vampire-like speed.

"She needs her spell candy," I told the Nightblood.

Chloe slipped one arm under Shea's legs and another behind her back, scooping her up into her arms.

"Hey, girl. You did good." Chloe shoved a lozenge in her mouth. I hadn't even seen her grab it from her pocket.

The second it hit Shea's tongue she perked up. "Hey."

We exited the space quickly, and then I was in Lincoln's arms. He somehow managed to tuck me into his body while keeping my torn arm from getting further injured, and still getting a good glare in at the guard.

"Be ready for the next fight in twenty minutes," the guard barked at our retreating backs.

I'd been stabbed in the arm, almost lit on fire, Sera was unusable, and Shea's ear was hanging off. I was not looking forward to seeing how the next six fights went.

"I used the dark magic," I admitted, breathing against Lincoln's neck.

"It's okay. Do whatever you have to do." Regardless of his words, I could hear the disappointment in his voice.

He ferried our small group over to a corner, where he started to work on healing my arm.

"No, Shea first." I pushed his hand away.

His brow furrowed and he opened his mouth to retort.

"No. Her ear is hanging off. Shea first," I repeated. "I'll work on myself a little. Noah taught me how to self-repair last week."

Lincoln frowned. "It depletes your energy."

I pointed to my best friend. "I'll take one of her energy lozenges."

Shea waved in front of my man's face. "Hello? Ear falling off."

Lincoln sighed, lighting up his hands and dousing Shea with the sunflower-colored magic. He looked tired, his normally upright posture slouched, sweat shining on his forehead while he winced as if in pain.

"Any tips for us?" I asked him as I started to rev up my own magic.

I'd set Sera on the floor so she could hopefully cool off inside of my cuff.

Lincoln nodded. "Yeah, you both need to be quicker, fight dirtier, and you should've killed that bitch. She nearly set you on fire," he barked.

"Gee, is that all?" I should have known my lover would never go easy on me. Not if it meant protecting me, and teaching me how to protect myself.

"I sent Luke to watch the other fights. They aren't making other people put weapons in the middle," he added.

"Yeah, I'd figured that." My voice shook a little as the pain in my arm transferred into my hand. Self-healing was doubly painful, and I was a total newbie, so I needed to take it slow. My one goal was to stop the bleeding and form a thin scab. Noah said small healing goals were good and attainable, so I wouldn't be worrying about tendons and ligaments and all that.

Stop bleeding, form a scab.

Shea's face finally relaxed; Lincoln had taken a good chunk of the pain, I could tell.

"Oh, I forgot something," he said.

"Hmm?"

How could there be more?

My boyfriend's cobalt blue eyes cut right through me. "Stay the hell away from that Abrus demon. He reeks of hellfire."

The second Lincoln said it, I knew Lucifer had sent the Abrus demon to watch over me. Goose bumps invaded every square inch of my skin, and I was reminded of James' prophecy. The one they apparently told at Tainted Academy. A far cry from the one our sweet Raphael believed in.

I pinned my eyes on the ceiling, praying for the first time in forever.

God, let me get through this night alive and end up in Angel City by morning.

With my mom.

And all my limbs.

Amen.

CHAPTER 18

Lincoln hadn't had time to heal me, as it had taken the entire break time just to re-adhere Shea's ear. I was exhausted after healing myself, but Shea's energy spell lozenge was akin to chugging three energy drinks. After taking them, I'd felt zippy and ready to throw down for the next two fights.

They went well. And by well, I mean I'd broken my pinky, probably needed some stitches in my left eyebrow, and was missing some hair from my ponytail, but we'd won. These kids were freaking badass scrappy hood kids. They knew how to survive, but so did we.

When we exited the cage of our third fight, Chloe and Luke were there, but no Lincoln.

"What's wrong?" I limped over to Chloe, whose

face was giving away that something bad had happened.

She immediately lost the 'something's wrong' face and smiled. "Oh, no big deal. Lincoln just…fainted, so my dad's guys took him back over the border."

"He fainted!" *Oh God. Maybe we overestimated how long the Celestials could be in Demon City.* How many hours had passed? I didn't know, but I was freaking exhausted.

Shea reached out a shaky hand and gave me one of those energy lozenges.

"Thanks." I popped it on my tongue and my heart jackknifed in my chest as the adrenaline shot through my body.

Limping to the corner that was now our healing space, I struggled to get to my chair. It was basically two chairs and a sleeping bag that had been set up for us. We were fighting every fight in the main cage, whereas other smaller fights were going on outside in the field. It was totally to exploit us. I'd also learned that freaking gray-haired Abrus demon was in charge of the night, and was the one donating the million dollars to the winner. He was front and center for every fight, watching me like a monster watches prey. My leg was killing me, my pinky hurt way more than you'd think a pinky could hurt, and there was no way I could see myself doing four more fights.

"Lincoln's calling," Luke said, then thrust his cell phone in my face.

I collapsed into the shitty picnic chair and grabbed the phone. "You okay?" I asked.

"I'm fine. Are *you* okay?" His voice sounded groggy.

No. I needed a five-hour nap, chocolate peanut butter ice cream, and a million dollars.

"Yeah, I'm okay," I lied.

"Listen, I sent another healer. She's going to cover the next two fights, and then Noah and I will come back for your big finish. You got this. We're bringing your mom home."

He sent a new healer? Who is it?

His pep talk totally made me cry, tears streaming down my cheeks as I fought to keep my emotions in check. "Everything hurts," I admitted.

He sighed. "I know. You need to reach that point where you're fighting with something other than your body. Your mind needs to take over. The hurt will heal, you just need to power through."

I wasn't sure what that meant, but it sounded legit.

"Okay."

"Brielle, I love you and I'm so proud of you." He sounded tired and defeated. I knew it was killing him not to be there with me every second. It would kill me to not be with him too.

"I love you too," I told him and hung up.

After taking a deep chug of water, I checked in with my best friend.

"How you doing? Lincoln said he's sending another healer for the next few fights, and he and Noah will come for the last two and fully patch us up."

She looked awful, bruised and bloody, probably how I'd look if I checked the mirror, but her spirit wasn't broken, that I could see. She hated this school, these asshole kids. They'd made their mark on her in her short time here, and she hadn't forgotten.

"I'm ready for a three-week vacation in Hawaii, but I'm good." She grinned and her healed lip cracked, dripping blood onto her teeth.

"Looks like you girls are in need of a healer," a familiar female voice trilled.

I spun in my seat to see Mrs. Greely standing there, clutching her tan purse and looking like a poodle in a pit bull shop.

"Mrs. Greely! You came." I stood and pulled her in for a hug even though it hurt. When she moved back, she smoothed my hair.

"Of course, dear. Raphael had to bribe the border guards a bit, but I'm here."

Raphael took part in bribing Demon City border guards? Now, that I would have paid to see.

Mrs. Greely made quick work of resetting and healing my pinky, then moved on to Shea's elbow. It was hit with some type of damaging spell. A ton of these students were Dark Mages, and they'd clearly been throwing premade spells their advanced teachers had crafted.

During my most recent fight, I'd squared off with a Centaur, hence the split eyebrow. He'd kicked me right in the face! We were lucky each competitor had submitted and we'd yet to have to kill anyone, but I doubted the entire night would go that way.

Shea leaned into me. "The others are getting tired too. We need to be explosive, go big right off the bat, and end these next few quickly."

It was a good plan, but harder when reality didn't pan out that way.

"What do you have in mind?" I mused, thinking she may have some plan to use our weapons. The announcer had stopped asking us to put them in the center of the room after it became obvious Sera was loyal to only me.

"Remember that black whip thing you did on the Succubus demon?" Shea recalled.

I shivered. I hated that I was using my dark magic to win these fights. It was also depleting my energy quickly.

"Yeah, assuming I can just *do* that again," I retorted.

"Next few fights, the second the buzzer sounds, just lash out with that whip. I'll create a magical shield of sorts to keep any spells from hitting us."

It was a good plan that hinged on me being able to just conjure up the whip like I did it all the time.

'*You don't need the whip. Let me at them and I'll cut them to pieces!*' Sera screamed.

216

I snickered to myself. I didn't like to admit it, but my dark magic was extremely easy to call forth now, so I was betting I could do it. Sera was amazing, but using her required me to get very close to my opponent to cause serious damage. I needed to save Sera's power for our final fight. She was susceptible to fatigue the same as me, and she wasn't getting power boost lozenges.

"Worth a try," I told Shea.

"Shall we bring our pretty angels back in the ring!" the announcer boomed.

He'd nicknamed us "angels," which couldn't be farther from the truth.

It hit me then, how messed up the world had become. We were participating in a televised fight to the death to win money that could buy a human being's slave contract back. As if a human should even be kept a slave in the first place.

"Good luck, girls. I'll try to stay as long as I can," Mrs. Greely stated, though already she looked positively green. No doubt this was her first time in Demon City.

What was so wrong with me that I could stand to live in Demon City without being affected? Shit, I'd even walked through Hell without much discomfort—what did that say about me as a person?

'It says your Lucifer powers allow it. That's all. Do you overthink everything?' Sera asked.

I groaned. 'Do you listen to all of my deeply

217

personal thoughts or just some of them?' I snapped back.

'Pretty much all of them. It's my only form of entertainment,' she retorted.

A chuckle escaped me, I couldn't help it.

"Come on, crazy lady." Shea dragged me up.

Whoops. I'd forgotten the task at hand. If I was ever stranded on a desert island and could only take one item, it would definitely have to be Sera. She'd amuse me until we both died of thirst.

'I don't drink water,' she interjected.

'Hush. It's go time,' I told my infinity weapon.

As we entered the ring, I relaxed a little. We were up against Steph and Ben. They looked beat, Steph holding a hastily wrapped hand to her chest and Ben limping. I guessed they weren't able to afford a healing demon.

They'd said they wouldn't fight us, not for real. But trust was a fickle thing. I didn't want to put my guard down too much, and then have them come out swinging full throttle.

As with the other times, the gate slammed, the fence electrified, and the buzzer sounded all within seconds. Just like that, the fight had begun.

Shea and I shared a look, and I decided to trust. Maybe it was because I wanted to embrace my lighter side and have faith. I didn't let the black whip come shooting out like I'd promised Shea. Instead I held Sera up and she shot a concentrated beam of light into Steph's thigh, making her drop to the ground screaming.

Ben burst forward and loosed an arrow at Shea's head, but it went over, missing her by mere inches.

Was that miss intentional?

I knew it would need to look real in order for them to save face after we left, but I didn't want to seriously injure them.

'*Don't hurt her too badly,*' I told Sera, and then my wings burst from my back and I launched into the air. The tips of my wings hit the edges of the cage, and a slight shock zipped through my shoulders.

Argh, freaking electrified fence!

I tucked my wings in a bit and sailed over Steph's crumpled form, landing behind her. Gripping her hair in my hand, I held Sera to her neck.

'*Just enough to draw blood,*' I instructed.

I felt Sera pull forward and nick Steph's throat, a single drop of blood falling.

"I submit!" Stephanie screamed.

The crowd booed. It was a short and easy fight, but I was grateful. I wanted to thank her, hug her, tell her my mom and I were so grateful.

Instead, I just lowered my knife, letting Ben scoop her up and walk away without even glancing in my direction.

A part of my childhood died then, watching my two old school friends walk out of a ring where I'd just tried to kill them. After the night was over, I'd never be coming back, and I'd probably never see Steph or Ben again.

I just hoped they knew how grateful I was.

———— • —— • ————

The next two fights were hell on my body and my mind. When the freaking psycho Necromancer and Beast Shifter we'd been fighting finally submitted, I burst into tears. The adrenaline surges and exhaustion were getting to me, and I could feel my sanity waxing and waning.

"We have a submission!" the announcer roared rather dully, like he wanted more blood.

The door to the cage burst open and the Necromancer and Beast Shifter scurried out, looking back at my black whip hand and me like I was the devil.

Shea's whimper in the corner drew my gaze to find her holding her chest. I glared at the Necro's back and went to help my friend.

"What's wrong?" I asked, tears streaming down my face.

"I think he chipped my collarbone," she gritted out.

I wanted to give up. I wanted to pick up my best friend, fly her out of there, and never speak of the day we'd entered this stupid fight again. I wanted to die.

220

"All right, fighters! One last fight left, between our sweet angel girls and two of the most powerful students we have at this school—Nadia and Gor!"

The color drained from Shea's face.

"What?" I breathed.

"It's the Dark Mage who beat up your brother and her Beast Shifter boyfriend. He's a panther," Shea replied.

I probably needed therapy, because at her words, I got excited. The girl who beat up my brother? The chick from the day we signed up for the fight? Oh, I was going to wipe the floor with her. I didn't care how bad I felt.

A blur of blond hair passed in front of me and then Noah's glowing golden hands were there, pulling Shea into his arms.

"Hey, baby." He winked at her.

She totally swooned, broken collarbone or not, and we left the cage.

"Where's Lincoln?" I asked excitedly. After Mrs. Greely surprised us by being able to stick it out and heal us for two fights, we'd agreed Lincoln and Noah should only come for the last round. They'd heal us up big-time right before, and then they would have enough energy to get us out of there when it was over. There was no way I could drive in the shape I was in at the moment.

Noah was pushing through the crowd to where Chloe and Luke were keeping our little ghetto healing

221

spot free. Some of Chloe's dad's Nightbloods were manning our corner like security guards manned the door of her dad's bar.

Noah didn't say anything. Did he not hear me?

"Noah, Lincoln said he would be here for the last fight. Is he okay?" Maybe the time he'd spent over here earlier had wiped him out too much.

"He's fine. He'll come when he can." Noah wasn't meeting my eyes. Something was wrong. Lincoln would never miss my final fight. *Ever*.

"Noah, whatever your last name is, you tell me everything right this instant." I grabbed his arm. *Hard*.

'*I'm very good at extracting information from people,*' Sera informed me.

Noah set Shea onto the sleeping bag and held his glowing hands over her collarbone. Then he looked behind me at the lingering demons and other general bad people and widened his eyes.

"Can you step into my office?" he said through clenched teeth.

Oh. It was a secret.

Every single muscle in my body, including the ones I didn't know I'd had before that day, screamed as I knelt next to him and leaned in to get as close as I could.

"What is it? I'm freaking out," I whispered.

Noah held my gaze for a moment, and I couldn't help but remark at how beautiful his green eyes were. "Someone...attacked your mom. Tried to kill her. He—"

A strangled cry left my throat and Shea gasped.

"Is she okay?" I managed. The room swam as I threatened to pass out. I'd been running on adrenaline since that morning, and it was finally catching up with me.

Noah reached out and grasped my hand. "She's shaken up but *totally* okay. She called Mikey, who called Lincoln. He's there now, and killed the demon that tried to hurt her. We just need you girls to win this fight as quickly as possible, so we can get your mom, and get the hell out of here."

My blood was boiling. The first thing that came to my mind was Grim. That motherfucker put a hit out on my mom so even if I won and transferred him the money, I wouldn't walk away happy. I felt it in my bones. It was *him*.

I'd been angry before at times in my life, but never had I been so livid. My wings snapped out of my back against my will, sending Chloe scurrying against the far wall.

"I'm going to kill him," I rumbled.

Noah looked at my wings, horrified. "Calm down. You're..."

"Smoking," Shea finished, pointing at my wings.

I glanced down at the tips of my wings to see black smoke curling off the ends.

Good.

Standing, I looked down at Shea. "Let's finish this."

You mess with my family, then you're going to get my full wrath.

CHAPTER 19

Nadia and Gor looked positively ready to throw down. They had tears in their clothes and some crusted blood on their body, but otherwise they looked injury free. They'd definitely had a healer demon at their disposal.

"What kind of name is that anyway? Gor?" I asked Shea as we made our way to the cage. I'd allowed Noah to do a little healing on me, but the rage and adrenaline were working wonders to keep me from feeling any pain.

The big hairy brute was disrobing, which meant he was probably going to—yep, he was shifting.

Awesome.

"It's short for Gordon. He's an asshole. I'm so

ready to kill them both, get Mom, and go home."
Shea grunted as we moved through the crowd.

Reaching out, I grabbed her hand and she turned to meet my gaze.

"Thank you. There's no one else I could count on for this."

Shea smiled and I ignored the blood on her teeth. "You're my ride or die, bitch. I love you."

I laughed and then winced. Add a broken rib to my list of maladies.

My eyes flicked to the black panther pacing the cage, as the crowd erupted in bloodthirsty screams.

"I'll take the Beast, you get the Mage?" I asked her. She was much more adept at handling a magic user than I was.

"Gladly," Shea responded, tightening her grip on the semicircular blades in her hands. Purple magic flowed from her wrists and surrounded the sharp edges.

We were both tired as hell and sore and...done. This needed to be a quick and ruthless fight—I wanted it to be, anyway—but something was nagging at my conscience. These were just kids. Or young adults. Whatever. They were fighting for money and a better station in life. Granted, they were all pretty much assholes and evil, but that was because they'd had to grow up here. This shithole Demon City didn't allow you to dream of anything else. They were doing the best they could with what they'd been given.

Oh God, what the hell am I doing? Softening my heart to these people right before I have to—

The buzzer sounded.

I was so conflicted that I wanted to throw up. Where were the new thoughts coming from?

The pink-haired Mage launched a purple ball of magic right at me and I dropped to the ground, rolling away from it. Seeing me on the ground, the panther decided to pounce.

'You're a good person. It's okay to feel sorry for them, but you also need to grab hold of your self-preservation, or we're about to die!' Sera yelped as the panther burst into the air and landed on top of me before I could get up.

She was right. What the hell was I doing having a crisis of conscience right now? I thrust Sera up into the animal's abdomen right as his jaw clamped around my right shoulder.

Sharp pain pierced my shoulder, and the panther and I both howled at the same time.

I had to put this moral dilemma out of my head and survive the match. My fight-or-flight system officially kicking in, I tucked my leg back as far as I could, wedged my boot underneath the panther's belly, and kicked out hard, launching him off me. He sailed across the space, taking Sera with him. I'd left her stuck in his gut. When he landed, he immediately pawed at her, ripping her out with one good swipe.

Plan B.

I didn't want to do this again. Using the dark magic so often was messing with me, making me feel hopeless and depressed whenever I called it up, but I didn't see any other way. With a deep breath, I called my black magic whip; it flared and grew out of my hand like a snake, and the crowd roared. The inky black energy that coursed along the edges of the whip sizzled as they made their way to the tip.

I reared my hand back, ready to flick the whip at the panther, when something red caught my eye. Too late, I turned to see a rosy spell crash into my chest. Shea screamed in frustration, and launched herself at the Mage while I was overcome with dizziness.

Shit.

Plan C.

The cage was spinning, and suddenly I wasn't sure if the panther before me was truly there or off to my right. Maybe my left. Either way, he was stalking closer, and I felt like I was falling over. I spread my legs apart in an effort to steady myself, and lashed out at the spot where I thought the animal was. I missed. He was still coming at me.

I didn't want to risk hurting Shea, so I backed up a bit farther to give myself a moment to gather my thoughts, my wings hitting the electric fence. Again. A cry of frustration left my throat, and I sucked my wings back into my body. Lashing out again, I was rewarded with a panther's yelp as my whip connected with something.

"Dizzy spell, Shea!" I shouted, hoping that made sense to her. I didn't have the energy to form complete sentences. Suddenly, two purple glowing balls flew through the air and crashed into me. Shea's magic. My vision cleared at once, just in time to see the panther arc through the air, jaw open and teeth glistening with saliva.

I flicked my wrist, wrapping the whip securely around his neck in one quick movement. When I tightened the hold, he cried out, falling to the floor.

'Cut his head off!' Sera shouted.

His catlike green eyes bored into me and I faltered.

"I don't want to kill you, but I will," I shouted, pulling the whip tighter as puffs of smoke rose from around his neck.

At my declaration, the whip started to slowly turn white. A bright Celestial glowing fire left my palm, and pulsed down the whip, changing its color.

'What the hell is that?' I asked Sera, hoping she was seeing this even though she didn't have eyes, and was on the floor in the corner.

'Angel fire. Just as deadly. I told you that you didn't need your dark magic.' I detected pride in her voice.

I'd called up Celestial magic! I didn't have to be dark, or use dark magic to be a badass!

The white fire licked down the rope, alarmingly close to his face.

"We submit!" Nadia screamed, her voice was heavy with defeat.

The victory buzzer sounded and the cage door opened.

We'd won.

Shock ripped through me as I called the whip back, letting it fall away from the panther's neck.

My mom was free, and we'd freaking won. I'd never have to come back to this wretched place again. I wanted to cry, I wanted a nap, I wanted so many things.

I sagged against the now unelectrified wall of the cage in relief.

My eyes tracked the Abrus demon, the silver-haired man entered the cage holding a tablet.

"Congratulations, ladies. Where would you like the money to be sent?" He was beaming with pride, and it was bothering the hell out of me.

He's happy to give me a million dollars and watch me go back to Angel City? Why?

His eyes flicked to the corner of the cage where Sera lay. Using the trick Michael taught me, I called her to me. She floated across the cage and into my hand.

The demon's left eyebrow raised, and a smile quirked the edge of his lips.

I pulled out the card I'd kept in my pocket that had Grim's bank details on it.

"You can send the money here," I said, handing him the information.

He took the card and then met my gaze. "I'll give you ten million each to leave Angel City, and work for me."

Ten million *each*? Who had that kind of money? What did this guy do for a living? I had so many questions, but I also *really* didn't want to know.

Shea's eyes grew dollar signs. "Like ten million up front right now?" my bestie asked.

I cut her a glare and shook my head. "No."

Short simple answer, I wanted to get the hell out of there, and see my mom.

The Abrus demon looked disappointed, but typed a few things out on his keypad, and then stepped closer to me, handing me the card back while leaning forward. "The Dark Prince is very pleased with your progress. He hopes to see you soon." He whispered in my ear, pulled away, and winked.

Ew. How dare he wink at me? Winks were for Noah and Lincoln, no one else. Well, maybe Archangel Michael, but that was it.

The demon walked away then, taking the stench of brimstone with him, or I would have given him a piece of my mind.

The Dark Prince is pleased with me? He hopes to see me soon? Pretty much everything I didn't want to hear had come out of that man's mouth.

'Forget it. You're safe now. Get to Lincoln and your mom!' Sera reminded me of my priorities.

Noah burst into the cage out of nowhere. "Grim

got the money. Let's get the hell out of here. People are pissed Fallen Academy won, and I doubt they'll keep it to themselves for much longer."

Yikes.

I glanced at my shoulder, which was mangled and bleeding freely. Using Sera, I cut the bottom half of my right pant leg off and handed it to Noah to make a quick dressing. He infused it with his orange healing light to staunch the wound, and then we were hobbling as fast as we could, Chloe and Luke on our heels.

"My dad's crew got kicked out," Chloe whispered.

"What?" I fired back. "Why?"

"They don't want any Angel City peeps in here anymore," she called back, and I noticed for the first time that she was wearing a red demon slave tattoo. So was Luke.

My mouth dropped open in horror and she grinned. "Chill. It's lip liner," she said in a low voice.

Oh thank God.

We were lost in the throng of demons, and Tainted Academy students heading across the parking lot when someone shouted.

"It's the Fallen Academy douchebags! They think they're better than us, and now they've taken our money!" an obviously drunk old man bellowed.

I looked up ahead to see they were surrounding our car. *Shit.*

"Back up!" Noah roared, pulling his blade, which glowed a fiery orange.

No one moved.

I did a quick head count and decided there were about fifty people blocking our way to the car.

'*Got any ideas?*' I asked Sera.

'*Show your boobs?*' she offered.

How did this weapon have anything to do with angels? She had a dirtier mind than me.

"Let's show them how Demon City really fights!" another person yelled.

The mob mentality kicked in, one person rushing us before they all flew forward.

My wings burst out at the same time as Noah's, a strangled cry leaving my throat as it ripped open my shoulder wound.

We were going to have to fly everyone out of the city. I'd flown Shea around before in a practice run; I'd gone ten feet up and then dropped her. It was really hard, yet I thought I might be able to do it again. But there was Luke and Chloe too, and we were about to get mauled.

Suddenly, a bright blue light flared in the sky and everyone stopped, covering their eyes.

A loud thump sounded nearby, and I looked up to see Archangel Michael standing on the roof of our SUV, glowing and looking gloriously fit for battle.

"Lincoln said you might need an escort," he boomed, his voice carrying across the parking lot. "Anyone who gets in the way of these five leaving, is going to spend some time in Hell," Michael barked, his sword shooting out a blue ball of fire that had everyone scattering and screaming.

"Holy shit," Chloe breathed.

"I love him," Shea exclaimed.

'You should smell him. He smells so good,' Sera chimed in.

"Get in the car!" Noah ordered.

The mob had parted like the Red Sea as Michael stood atop our SUV, sword raised.

My boyfriend called Archangel Michael to bail me out so he could stay and protect my mom.

Oh my God, I am so marrying him one day.

Once we were all in, Noah threw the car in Reverse and peeled out of the parking lot. I leaned out the window and looked up.

"Michael is flying above our car!" I told my friends.

"He *is* the patron saint of safe travel," Luke chimed in, trying to get a view from where he sat, smooshed between Chloe and Shea.

I opened the center console, where I'd stashed my cell phone, and dialed Lincoln.

"I saw everything on TV. I'm so glad you're okay," he said in a rush as soon as he answered.

"How's my mom?" I tried not to panic, but my shaky voice betrayed me.

"I'm fine, honey." My mom's voice was laced with fear, I could hear it. Something had scared the shit out of her however long ago, and she was *still* scared.

"We're only a few blocks away," I told them. "Michael is escorting us," I added, so they wouldn't worry.

"All right, we'll meet you outside. Is there anything else you want to take from here?" Lincoln's voice was full of concern, and it only hit me then that we were permanently leaving my home and all its possessions. I had all the pictures of my dad that I wanted, plus clothes and bedding. None of the other stuff mattered. After what happened in the parking lot, I didn't think we should linger.

"No. Let's just get my mom out of here," I told him.

Noah pulled up to the curb of my old apartment building, and I glanced over to see he was looking quite ill. Sweaty and pale.

"You okay?" I asked.

He just nodded, mouth turned down in a grimace.

Wasting no time, I jumped out of the car, but when my eyes fell on Bernie's tent, my heart stopped.

Bernie.

I heard the door open behind me and Shea stumbled out.

"Oh God. Who is going to take care of Bernie?" she whispered.

Since we'd moved to Demon City, we'd always taken care of Bernie and Max. Always. I couldn't remember a night when my mom, Shea, my brother, or I didn't bring down a cup of hot soup, a bagel, or something for him. He was one of those misunderstood people. No drug problem, no criminal record, just a guy who was human and couldn't hold a job in a magical world.

"We are." My voice was firm.

He wasn't a demon slave. We were taking him with us.

I approached the tent and could see his shoes were off, feet sticking out.

"Is that you, Brielle?" Before I got too close, his sweet voice rang through the space. He peeked his head out, and Maximus barked in excitement.

"Yeah, Bernie, it's me. Long time no see." Bending down, I patted Max's head and poked my head inside the tent. He had a little setup in there that would take quite a while to break down.

"You okay? You smell of blood." Bernie frowned.

I swore the guy had the nose of a bloodhound.

"Got in a little fight, but I'm all right. Hey, Bernie? My mom's moving to Angel City, and I'd like you and Max to come with us there. I can't explain much right now, but we don't have time to pack all your stuff."

His mouth popped open in surprise. "They don't like my kind in the fancy part of town."

My kind. *Homeless*. Anger flared within me at his words. The high-and-mighty fallen were always looking down on these sorts of "unsightly" things. What kind of angel blessed were you, if you couldn't reach out to those in need?

Lincoln and my mom burst from the back door then. The moment Lincoln saw me stooped down, talking to Bernie, a dawning came over his face. He knew what I was doing.

"I've still got my trailer. It's all his if he wants it," Lincoln offered.

Tears leaked from my eyes. *When did I become such a crier?*

"You hear that, Bernie? A silver Airstream just for you and Max, what do you say?" I started to grab his backpack, when he reached out and grasped my wrist lightly.

"I say thank you, Brielle. Thanks for thinking of me. And I'd love to."

His hand on my wrist was vibrating, like a high-pitched buzzing, sending soothing vibrations up my arm and into my injured shoulder. Before I could think more on it, he let go.

My mom sidestepped Lincoln and gave Shea and me both a gentle hug, which hurt because my body was falling apart. Lincoln propped open the stairwell door, and we started to grab my mother's boxes and suitcases.

"I've got a dead Abrus demon and three Snakeroot demons locked in the bathroom up there, so we need to leave, *now,*" Lincoln told us as he heaved Bernie into a standing position.

A dead Abrus demon! I didn't even want to know the details. Not right now.

We opened the back of our large three-row SUV and packed Maximus in the cargo hold, with all of my mom's stuff.

I'd forgotten about Michael, until he started to descend, and landed lightly on the roof of the car.

"Can you take it from here, Lincoln? I feel sick being in this energy for too long," he called out to my boyfriend.

Lincoln nodded. "Yes. Thank you, sir."

Interesting. Even the Archangels can't be here for too long.

Michael's gaze snapped to Bernie and a knowing smile lifted his lips. Before I could think any more about it, he was gone, a glowing white dot in the sky.

As we drove away from my home in Demon City, I looked back for the last time at the place that had ruined our lives. My father died here, and my mother and I were enslaved here. There was nothing about this place I wanted to remember.

CHAPTER 20

"OH, HONEY, ARE YOU SURE IT'S NOT TOO MUCH of a hassle having me here? I can stay at a hotel for a few days until I find a job."

My mother was standing in Lincoln's kitchen. She looked overwhelmed and grateful, but also in shock. The second we'd driven over the border, her slave mark had disappeared from her forehead, which was a part of the contract we'd made Grim sign. It was also why he tried to kill her before she'd crossed the border.

Lincoln waved a hand in dismissal. "Not a hassle at all. To be honest, I'm hoping you'll cook for me. I've missed home-cooked food. Brielle never makes me anything," he pouted.

My mom grinned. "Yes, I'm afraid my cooking skills rubbed off on Mikey more. Brielle is more like her father—a good eater."

Haha! I laughed but then held onto my ribs. Even though I'd spent a few hours in the healing clinic, after dropping Bernie and Maximus off at their new digs, I was still in a shitload of pain and felt like I could sleep for a year.

"Honey, why don't you go lie down. I'd like to keep an eye on you over the next few days, make sure you heal okay," my mother trilled.

"Yes," Lincoln agreed. "Come on." He started to walk me into his bedroom and then stopped.

"Er," I mumbled and started to turn around.

'*Oh my God, I should lie down in my mom's bed, right?*' I asked Sera.

Before my weapon could answer, my mom held up her hands. "Please. We're all adults here. Brielle is twenty now. I don't mind."

My cheeks went bright red with embarrassment. My mom was always cool like that. For my fifteenth birthday, she gave me condoms and a pack of birth control, even though I wasn't having sex.

"Right," I squeaked and shuffled into Lincoln's room. There was *no* way I was having sex with her in the other room, but I wouldn't mind sleeping next to Lincoln. I fell into bed, careful not to land on my bad shoulder, though pain started to flare up everywhere else as my joints settled.

"You did it, Bri. You got your entire family out of Demon City." Lincoln's voice was soft in my ear, his fingers trailing along my skin.

I had. I'd saved my family.

It was a beautiful thought. A huge relief.

Which was why it surprised me to fall asleep with such happiness, and wind up sucked into such a nightmare.

I was walking through that alleyway in Hell, and all of the demons were surrounding Sera. But Sera wasn't a cactus. She was a small child, and that old lady was there again, screaming. Everyone slowly turned to look at me, smiling and welcoming me like I was home. I was sweating profusely, looking for a portal or a way home.

Then Lucifer showed up and he started to train me, just like James said. We worked on my dark magic, and I was a willing student. It was awful. In the dream, I would do as he told me, but in my head, I knew it was wrong.

I wanted out.

But I was stuck in Hell.

"Brielle!" Lincoln's voice jarred me from my sleep and my eyelids snapped open. It was the fourth time he'd woken me that night.

I looked over to the clock, and saw it was seven in the morning. I didn't want to fall back asleep, even though I was exhausted, I couldn't risk being sucked back into the nightmares.

"You're soaking wet." He touched my back gingerly.

"Nightmares," I croaked.

Lincoln's dark eyebrows were drawn together with concern. "What about?"

I didn't want to make a habit of lying to Lincoln, and I had yet to tell him about what James had said. Sitting up, I hugged my knees. "Hell. Lucifer. General bad things."

Lincoln sighed. "Okay. Well, you used a lot of your dark magic. You took off the necklace. All of that was probably too much for you."

Remembering the necklace still in my jeans pocket, I nodded. Reaching down, I pulled it out, heavy in my hand. "Will you?" I asked him and lifted my long blonde hair.

He took the necklace from me. As he was coming over my head with it, it laid against my chest and… cracked.

The sound was unmistakable. I gasped, looking down to see the crystal split right down the middle.

"What does that mean?" I turned to my boyfriend.

Lincoln looked scared for the tiniest second before it vanished. "Nothing. We'll just have Mr. Claymore make a new one."

Nodding, I reached for his hand. "I have to tell you something, but I need you to not freak out."

His hand tensed, eyes widened. "Okay."

He was totally going to freak out.

'*As he should*,' Sera piped up from her place on the floor.

'*Not helping*.'

"So...my old friend from Demon City is Sighted." I let that sentence linger. The Sighted were so freaking rare that knowing one was akin to being besties with one of the fallen archangels.

"And?" His hand was starting to sweat in mine.

I gave a nervous laugh. "And I saw him at the fight. He told me he sees a different prophecy for me."

Lincoln breathed in and out deeply. "Which is?"

I chewed my lip and decided to just blurt it out. "I go to the underworld and train with Lucifer to use my dark magic."

Lincoln's eyes widened so far, I thought they might fall out of the sockets. "*What!* That's ridiculous!"

"I know!" I told him. "It's just as ridiculous as Raphael's prophecy that I'll go down there, and kill Lucifer."

Lincoln was silent.

I shifted uncomfortably. "You don't think I'm going to actually do that, right?"

He did. I could see it in his face. "I don't want you to. It's too dangerous. But..."

I swallowed hard, my heart rate starting to pick up speed. "But?"

Lincoln stroked my thigh with his thumb. "But you have these incredible powers, and black wings, you even went into Hell to get Sera and it didn't seem to affect you. If anyone could do it, and end this war…it's you."

Oh my God, he drank the Kool-Aid. "Lincoln, I'm not doing that." I stood. "I want to be normal. I just got my family all together, and now I want to focus on my healing studies, and help out with the war in that way," I declared.

He nodded, dropping the subject. "Okay." But his words, his curt nod, and stiff body language didn't match up.

He actually expected me to kill Lucifer?

The smell hit us both at the same time.

"What's that?" Lincoln's brows knit together in confusion.

I grinned. "*That* is my mom's cinnamon-banana walnut waffles."

Lincoln wiped his mouth. "I just drooled a little."

Laughter erupted out of me, and I decided to let the whole killing Lucifer thing go. For now.

"How do you feel?" he asked, as I limped across the room, and made my way into the bathroom to brush my teeth.

"Like I got hit by a bus," I assured him.

Make no mistake, I'd be walking funny for weeks.

———— · ————

When we'd finally made our way out to the kitchen,

I grinned at the sight of Shea, Mikey, and Noah sitting around the table, shoving their mouths full of waffles, piled high with cubes of butter, and maple syrup.

"Hey, bro. I didn't know you'd be here." I gave Mikey a side hug. He spent most of his weekends with his pack on Clark's land. He was still learning to control the beast, but quick side hugs were okay.

"Are you kidding? Mom's home, so I had to come." He was wearing a goofy lopsided grin.

Mom's home. Those two words hit me with the realization of what had happened. I'd gotten my mom out.

"I'm going to need more batter. Especially if we want to take some to Bernie," my mom declared.

"Oh, I've hooked Bernie up," Lincoln replied, eyeing the piping-hot waffle coming out of the chipped red maker, my mom brought from home.

I looked at my boyfriend. "Oh really?"

He chuckled. "I told Raph about the situation. He said it's no problem for Bernie to come to the cafeteria and eat after the students have eaten their meals—before they've put everything away."

My mom met my eyes, and I could see she was totally planning our wedding in her head.

"That was very sweet of you, Lincoln. Thank you," she told him.

I smiled, getting on my tippy toes to kiss his cheek. "Thank you."

Lincoln's cheeks were red, and he mumbled a "you're welcome" to both of us.

My mom held up a dish towel. "Hang on, you call him Raph? The Archangel of Healing?"

Lincoln chuckled. "Yeah, it felt weird at first, but he asked us to. He doesn't want to seem above anyone. He's a friend."

He is a friend. A very good friend.

My mom started to tear up, looking down at the floor.

"Oh, Mom, what's wrong?" I crossed the kitchen to be by her side.

She wiped the tears and patted my hand. "Nothing. I'm just...happy. I haven't been happy in a long time."

Silence descended upon the kitchen. I knew she'd had it hard in Demon City after I'd left, then doubly hard when Mikey was having his issues. Now I could see the stress it had caused her. Close up, she looked tired with bags under her eyes, hair limp and dull.

"Lots more happy days ahead, Mom," I assured her.

Lincoln stepped in front of us. "Absolutely, but only if I get one of those waffles right now."

My mother's laughter filled the space around us, and my chest felt lighter and lighter as each person joined in.

This, our little family moment right here, was one of the happiest days of my life.

CHAPTER 21

THE NIGHTMARES DIDN'T STOP.

Six weeks of never-ending nightmares. Hell. Demons. Lucifer.

It was awful, and I'd turned into an insomniac because of it. I did anything to avoid sleep now—coffee, energy drinks, going for late-night walks. I just didn't want to be sucked back into that place. It was making me scared to close my eyes. It all felt so real.

And to top off that shit storm, my mom couldn't find a job. Apparently there was no room for a Necromancer in Angel City—other than tending to dead flowers and decorating cakes, but those jobs were given to Necros who grew up in the city, and graduated from the academy. My mom having been a raiser of the dead in Demon City was akin to having a criminal record.

The one good thing going on in my life at the moment was Bernie. He was thriving. He'd put on some weight, looked clean and happy with his daily showers and shave. Raphael had even given him a small job folding sheets and towels. After the school maids washed them, they'd drop them off at Bernie's trailer, and he'd fold them. He said it gave him a purpose, but the only drawback was trying to keep Maximus off the clean folded sheets.

Now, I was being called to Raphael's office between lunch and battle class. I didn't know what it was about, but I hoped I wasn't in trouble.

After knocking on the door, Raphael called out for me to enter. Pulling the big heavy door back, I stepped inside to see him standing at his desk.

I smiled. "Hey."

Please don't be in trouble for something.

"Hello, Brielle. How are you healing?" Raphael asked kindly.

Okay, that didn't seem like something you'd ask someone in trouble.

I rolled out my shoulder, which had healed weeks ago. "Great, sir. Thank you."

He chuckled. "Oh, come on. It's coming on two years now that we've been friends. You can call me Raph or Raphael. All the other students do."

I sighed in relief. "So, I'm not in trouble?"

He frowned. "Of course not. Why would you…? Oh, right."

He seemed to just now realize he'd called me to his office in the middle of the day.

"I wanted you to come by because the Fallen Army is giving Lincoln a promotion, and it's a surprise. I know he'd like you there when it's announced. It's this Saturday. He thinks he's going to be giving a fellow comrade an award, but really I'll be promoting him to captain."

My heart nearly burst with pride. Lincoln was one of the most deserving people I knew. He took his job seriously, and was completely dedicated to the war beyond the city's walls.

"Of course I'll be there." I smiled so wide, that I thought my face might crack.

Raphael beamed, and his wings glowed a honey color as his mood seemingly lifted.

"Perfect! You'll need to be there at six sharp. I'll have a table for you and his friends, Noah, Darren, and Blake. Lincoln's been through a trying few years, and having you all there to cheer him on will mean the world to him."

He *had* been through a trying few years, and the fact that Raphael had asked me to be at his table meant the world to me.

"It'll be amazing," I assured him and eyed the door. I needed to get to battle class.

"Before you go…" Raphael took in a deep breath

and stood, crossing the room in elegant strides that would make a cheetah look clumsy. "Lincoln told me about the nightmares."

Great. Lecture time.

The nightmares were absolutely horrible, and now when I drifted off, I was so full of fear that I'd jerk awake mere seconds later, heart pumping with adrenaline. Maybe Lincoln was right to tell Raphael.

"Sit down. I'll give you a note to excuse you from class," Raphael offered.

I sighed and dropped my bag, collapsing onto the couch.

"Why do you think you're having the nightmares?" he quizzed, sitting cross-legged on the ground in front of me, wings outstretched behind him. He was so casual, it felt like we were just two old friends having a little chat.

I didn't keep many things from Raphael. Mostly, he knew about my dark magic whip and everything that had happened with Sera in Hell. He was easy to talk to, and never judgmental.

I fingered the pendant around my neck. It was a new one Mr. Claymore had made for me to replace the cracked one, but it didn't work as well as the first one did. I hadn't been able to produce anything even close to a Celestial orb.

"I think when I took the necklace off to get Sera… my dark magic took hold and… I dunno, I guess it's in control now." I needed to talk to someone about this, and Raphael was the best person to share my true feelings with.

"Wrong," he admonished. "You are in control, always. You just need to work on a few things."

I groaned. "Like what?"

Raphael gave me one of his loving looks, the one that usually preceded some hard-to-hear advice.

"That dark magic you house, dies out quickly in the presence of Celestial light, which you are consumed with."

I chewed my bottom lip, my heart thumping wildly. It reminded me of what Michael had said, that I had the brightest light he'd ever seen in a human, but that the darkness was akin to a moth being attracted to a flame. "Then why is my dark magic still...alive and well?"

If it couldn't be sustained in the presence of the Celestial light, then what the hell?

Raphael looked up at me sadly. "Because you constantly feed it with resentment and anger. So much resentment, it's making you sick. It's feeding the powers you inherited from the Dark Prince," Raphael stated, staring at my chest like some alien was about to pop out.

I frowned. "Resentment at wh—"

"Me, for not healing your father. The world. Angel City. God. Everyone who let you down, and let your father die."

Raphael's words ripped open my chest, a physical

pain pinched my heart, and I gasped. Tears started to trickle down my cheeks as every repressed emotion I'd held bubbled to the surface.

"Why didn't you?" I shouted suddenly. "You're the archangel of fucking healing, and you didn't even touch him!"

My words turned to short sobs and I realized how badly I'd wanted to ask him. He was there in the hospital when my father had been undergoing the initial tests. He was always at the hospitals, praying for people and trying to comfort them, but not once had I heard of him healing anyone.

Raphael looked at the floor. "For purely selfish reasons. If I heal anyone in a miraculous way, I can't go home." The way he said home was heartbreaking, like he longed so much to go back to where he came from. Mr. Claymore had alluded to something similar, but to hear Raphael say it was crazy.

I sank back farther into the couch.

"What?" That was asinine. Once again, I wanted to inform him that he was the Archangel of Healing. How could he carry that title if he never actually *healed* anyone?

Raph shook his wings a little, as if shaking off old memories. "It is my penance for starting the fallen war." His voice was so soft I wasn't sure I'd heard him right.

"Wait... Y-you started the war?" Now I was sitting forward so far, I was afraid I might fall off.

"I heard in Fallen history class that Lucifer tried to break into Heaven with his demons, and you and the other angels met them halfway, stopping them."

Raphael nodded. "Partly true. Lucifer first came to Earth with his demons, and started to terrorize the humans. I...left my home without permission and intervened. Against free will."

My mouth popped open. Free will was super important to the four archangels. The way Raphael said it made it sound like he'd committed a heinous crime.

I was enthralled. "Then what happened?"

Raphael ran a hand through his hair. "My best friends followed me down here, and fought by my side, thus starting the fallen war."

Whoa. "But if you hadn't come down here, humanity would be completely enslaved by Lucifer!"

Raphael arched one eyebrow slightly, like maybe that wasn't the truth. "Lucifer was once my friend. Did you know that?" he asked me.

Now that *did* shock me. "I knew he was an angel too once."

Raph nodded, staring out the window, seemingly lost in old times. "I should not have robbed humanity of the spiritual development they would gain from fighting Lucifer on their own, for they are more than capable."

His words gave me chills. *Humans? They're the weakest race alive.*

"No. They're not weak."

Freaking mind reader.

"But you were helping!" I defended him.

He sighed. "Part of me was helping, but part of me wanted to get back at my old friend for leaving. Show him how powerful I was, how capable of protecting the humans I was. I fought out of anger and resentment."

"Oh." I sat back. Yikes, that didn't sound good. It sounded quite familiar, actually.

He shook his head. "And so to prove his power, instead of the dozen or so demons he'd brought up to Earth that night, Lucifer unleashed thousands, and we fought. We infected humanity, and it was all my fault."

I slid off the couch and knelt before the fallen angel. His whole body was sunken in, his expression defeated.

Grasping his hands, I looked into his deep blue eyes. "I forgive you." Those words seemed to unlock something in my chest, and a sob racked me from head to toe. "For my dad, for the war, for all of it. I forgive you."

His face contorted as he seemingly held back tears. Then the angel's arms came up and embraced me in a hug. I suddenly felt lighter, as if a fifty-pound weight I'd been carrying all this time, had finally fallen off.

When we pulled back, I saw we were both

crying. I laughed and wiped my eyes. "I have so many more questions, so many things I don't understand."

Like if the other side, or Heaven, was so great, then why did they come here at all?

Raphael chuckled. "There is nothing I could say to answer those questions that your earthly mind would understand fully. It's hard to comprehend on this side of the veil."

The veil. They'd referred to that in my fallen history class. It meant while I was alive, I wouldn't understand. When I died and crossed the veil to the other side, all would be revealed, or some philosophical shit along those lines.

"Okay, one more question." I held up a finger.

Raphael smiled. "Okay."

"Is reincarnation real? Because growing up we had a dog, Pepper, that drowned. Yet, not a year later we got a new puppy, and it had all the same mannerisms and personality. I swear it was the same dog, so we named it Salt."

Raphael chuckled good-naturedly. "Yes, of course reincarnation is real. You think you can figure it all out, and learn your soul's lesson in one tiny human lifetime?"

Whoa. My mind was blown.

'*This is intense. Ask him if Michael has a human wife,*' Sera commented. I nearly jumped, having forgotten she was with me.

255

"Does Michael have a human wife?" I blurted out the rumor about the most popular archangel.

Raph's eyes glittered. "Are you going to keep my answer confidential?"

My mouth popped open. "He does?"

The archangel nodded. "And a daughter."

What! "How old is she? Where do they live? How long have they been married? Is his daughter human or—"

Raphael's belly laugh stopped me in my tracks. "I think it's time you got back to class." He stood swiftly, pulling me up by the hands as he did.

Damn, I was so close to learning all of the answers to life's most sought-after questions.

Raphael patted my shoulder. "Some of life's most satisfying answers come from things we learn ourselves."

Ugh. Boring.

My eyes bugged suddenly as a new thought came to me. "Was my dad reincarnated? Is he a kid walking around somewhere on Earth?"

Raphael smiled again and shrugged. "Probably not. He'd want to wait for your mother before reincarnating again, since they're soul mates."

The wind was knocked out of me at that simple yet sweet declaration. *Are.* He'd said they "are" soul mates, not "were." Like my dad wasn't really dead.

"Of course," I muttered, trying to hold my shit together. I'd cried way too much for one visit.

I grabbed my bag as Raphael scribbled a note for me. When he handed it to me, he beamed. "Brielle, may you sleep soundly tonight."

And I did. I slept without any dreams at all, just a deep, restful sleep, and a knowing that the darkness within me was no longer being fed.

It had actually retreated.

CHAPTER 22

IT WAS FRIDAY MORNING, THE DAY BEFORE Lincoln's big shindig, and I awoke to a grinning Shea hanging over my bed with a note.

"Geez! You scared me." I shrank back into my pillow as her psycho grin ramped up a notch.

"This was slid under our door in the early hours," she squealed.

I sat up, yawning, and plucked the envelope from Shea's grasp. It was some thick fancy cardstock, and when I pulled it out, I grinned, recognizing the handwriting immediately.

What: The most epic, random date night of your life.

When: Tonight. 7.

Why: Because I love you.

"Am I stupid smiling?" I asked Shea, who was peeking over my shoulder.

She nodded. "Totally."

I sighed. "Why is he so perfect?"

Shea shrugged. "I don't know, but Noah could take some notes in the romance department. His idea of a date night is watching old *Predator* movies, and winking at me while we eat stale popcorn."

I chuckled. "But you've finally had sex."

She swooned and fell on her bed. "Finally. And it's amazing, and I think we're going to win the sex Olympics."

I laughed so hard my stomach started to hurt. "How am I supposed to get through classes today knowing Lincoln is taking me on some special date!" I stood and started to rifle through my closet, looking for the perfect outfit to wear tonight.

"I'd say we should ditch, but today we learn to shoot guns in weapons class, and no way in hell am I missing that," Shea declared.

"Totally," I agreed.

"And if I accidentally shoot Tiffany in the foot, oopsie," Shea added.

The Tiffany war was in full effect once again. She was constantly calling us nasty names, and trying to get in the way of our successes. Recently, she'd been party to helping Shea fail an important magical exam. That girl was downright evil.

"All right, I'm gonna shower. I'll see you at breakfast," I told my bestie.

She nodded and picked up the note Lincoln had sent. "You guys are lucky to have found each other."

We were. I focused on that thought all day.

———◆·◆———

Lincoln had rented a limo! He'd also hired private security to shadow us to the fanciest restaurant in Angel City.

As we waited for the check, he peered at me with his crystalline blue eyes. "One more stop before we head home, okay?"

We could make ten more stops before home. I didn't care. This was the best night of my life. After he paid the bill and we climbed back into the limo, I watched as it headed away from the city I knew and into unfamiliar territory. Our SUV of security guards was right behind us.

"Where are we going?" I asked.

It was fully dark out now, and the streets and highways were hard to make out, especially since I hadn't exactly traveled around Angel City much.

He grinned at me devilishly. "You'll see."

Ugh. I wiggled in my seat. Patience was so not my virtue.

When the limo slowed and pulled up to two very

large, extremely familiar gates, my throat tightened with emotion.

Lincoln's hand slid across the seat and rested in mine with a squeeze. We were at the cemetery where my dad had been buried. I hadn't been there in years, not since we'd laid him to rest. The limo seemed to know just where to go.

"You've been talking to my mom a lot, I see."

He chuckled. "Perk of living with your mom, besides the food, is that she'll tell me anything I want to know about you."

My heart was fluttering like crazy in my chest.

The limo pulled right up to the area he was buried in, and I saw a strip of tea lights laid out, leading our path to his grave. Lincoln must have spent all day planning this.

He turned to me. "So, I've met your mom, your brother, and your best friend. I wanted to make it complete and meet your dad too."

Don't sob. You're cool. Keep your shit together.

Tears were leaking from my eyes as I tried not to let it turn into a full-on ugly cry.

'I'm totally crying too,' Sera offered.

'What? That's not possible,' I told her.

"I have yet to meet your family," I answered Lincoln.

He brushed my hair away from my shoulder. "Next weekend?" he asked, and I nodded.

Lincoln helped me out of the limo, and we walked

hand in hand along the tea lights to my father's grave, which was adorned with fresh flowers and a lantern.

"Hey, Dad," I whimpered, falling to my knees before his headstone.

I had so many amazing memories of this man. He was the even-tempered one, while my mom was the punisher. My dad was the silly one, always playing pranks and lightening my mom up because she was an overly serious worrier. My dad was a dreamer, a risk taker, a unique soul. We'd only had a fraction of the time together that we deserved, but enough for me to hang on to those precious memories.

I was scanning my father's headstone when I noticed something shiny on top of it. Shiny like a diamond.

My breath caught and I turned around to see Lincoln on one knee.

"Brielle, I know you're young, still in school, and you also have a lot of your life to live before settling down, but you and I are the same age my mom and dad were when he got her a promise ring, so I thought..." He looked nervously at the ring on the headstone. "This is my promise to you that when you're done with school, when you're ready, I will marry you and have a family with you, and try to make you happy for the rest of your life...if you'll have me."

I burst into ugly tears and threw myself at him, wrapping my arms around his neck, and peppering his face with wet kisses.

"Is that a yes?" he asked when I came up for air.

Laughter spilled out of me. "Yes. Hell yes!" I shouted.

Marry Lincoln one day and have his babies? Sign. Me. Up.

He reached over and pulled the ring from the top of the headstone, slipping it onto my finger. It was a delicate diamond baguette band with blue and white stones. It was perfect, he was perfect, and even though getting engaged in a cemetery might have been creepy to some people, this was perfect.

My fingers slipped through his hair, relishing in the moment. Nothing could ruin it for me. Not my stupid devil mark, not the two prophecies, nothing.

"Aw, isn't that sweet." Lucifer's voice dripped with sarcasm from behind me and I gasped.

Fear shot through my body, making my knees go weak. Before I could even process the voice I'd just heard, Lincoln burst into action, throwing me behind him and pulling his sword. I tumbled with the sudden movement and fell to the grass. Looking up, I saw the Prince of Darkness dressed in a three-piece suit, both arms fully attached to his body.

He grew his freaking arm back! The last time I saw it, Lincoln had hacked it off.

Our security team of four Fallen Army warriors now felt pathetically small. They'd obviously just realized what the hell was happening, and were running toward us with guns drawn.

Lucifer pulled a flaming orange sword, and with a gleam in his eye, he lunged at the love of my life. Lincoln dodged out of the way and brought his own glowing sword down on the Dark Prince's. Lucifer was battling Lincoln, sword against fiery sword, and I didn't like it. Not one bit. One wrong move and Lincoln could be gored to death.

Kicking off my high heels, I stood and gathered my magic within me, pulling on that fizzy light magic and letting it bubble to the surface. With a grunt, I thrust my hands outward, gathering all of the light magic I could, and then I pushed it outward. I pushed so hard, I felt dizzy. A huge Celestial orb flew from my hands, but it wasn't all white light like the one I'd produced in Mr. Rincor's classroom. This one was half golden yellow, half inky black.

Shit. I still had some anger and resentment to work through, and it was all toward the person before me. If you could even call Lucifer a person.

Bullets started to fly and I pulled Sera from my thigh holster.

'*Dip me in the light magic,*' she instructed.

Taking two steps forward, I slid Sera into the floating ball in the air, careful only to let the honey-colored light cover her blade.

The bullets suddenly stopped, and I peered over my shoulder to see a handful of upper-level demons had shown up to take care of our security detail.

No.

'That's my future husband,' I told Sera. *'Protect him.'*

Just then, black tentacles sprang from Lucifer's back and wrapped around Lincoln's body. He screamed in agony as they tightened around him, and I could hear the sound of snapping bones as Lincoln's wings were bent backward by the dark bands.

"No!" I shouted and aimed Sera at Lincoln. Identical tentacles, but of white light, leaped out from my blade and attached themselves to the black bands holding Lincoln. The white cords yanked at the black ones, loosening their hold on my love.

'Leave me. I'll protect him. You grab Lincoln's sword and fight,' Sera instructed.

She'd never led me astray before, so I let go of her, surprised to see she was able to keep herself hovering in midair on her own. Those golden light bands were breaking down the black ones that held Lincoln.

Seeing what I was doing, Lucifer suddenly detached from his black tentacles and made a run for me.

Bending down, I swooped up Lincoln's sword, and lunged to dip it in the Celestial orb I'd made. When I pulled it out, it was covered in twelve-inch bluish-golden flames.

Lucifer laughed behind me. "You think a little Celestial fire is going to kill me?"

I spun, holding the sword before me. Those black

eyes bored into mine, and I felt a sickness wash over me from head to toe.

"Let him go!" I shouted.

Lincoln was pulling at the cords, screaming in pain.

Lucifer smiled devilishly. "Done." He snapped his fingers and Lincoln fell to the ground. The bands had disappeared.

"Come with me. It's your destiny," the Prince of Darkness cooed, and just like that a portal opened behind him.

Not in a million freaking years.

My wings popped out of my back, and I slowly started to walk backward to Lincoln. I opened my free right hand and used the ability Michael had taught me, calling Sera to me. When I felt the cold steel in my palm, I wrapped my fingers tightly around her.

"I'm not going anywhere with you. *Ever*," I told the epic douchebag who'd just messed up my proposal.

Lincoln was now standing beside me—limping rather—and I handed him his sword.

Lucifer grinned. "It's really touching that you two think you can keep me from getting what I want."

A twig cracked behind me, and I peered over my shoulder to see half a dozen Castor demons and a few Hellhounds. Our guards looked either knocked out or dead, and it seemed one had even run off.

My stomach fell.

No. No one was taking Lincoln or me anywhere. The urgency of the situation pressed in on me, and something inside of me snapped. I thrust Sera forward and she shot a blinding light into the Dark Prince's face, causing him to yelp in surprise and cover his eyes. Then a white-hot whip of Celestial light flew from my palm and wrapped around the Devil's neck. I yanked and he fell forward, but only for a second before his wings burst from his back and then he was skyborne. With a jerk I was pulled up with him, hanging from the whip in my hand that was still around his throat.

Shit.

I pumped my own wings, trying to use the strength of my flapping to pull Lucifer back down to Earth.

"Brielle!" Lincoln shouted helplessly from the ground.

The Hellhounds howled and panic fully gripped me.

My flapping was no use. I was being dragged higher and higher, and when I looked up, I saw the Dark Prince was pulling on my whip like a rope, drawing me closer to him even though it seemed to be burning his hands.

'Let go. Fly to Fallen Academy,' Sera instructed.

I dissolved the whip as she told me to, and the loss of tension sent both of us flinging apart.

Using the momentum, I raced to the ground,

where Lincoln was throwing a Hellhound into the Celestial orb I'd created.

We weren't going to get out of here alive by driving, and I wasn't leaving Lincoln and his broken wings while I flew off to safety.

'*Oh no. Don't.*' Sera had obviously heard my thoughts.

When I was within arm's reach of my man, I hooked my hands underneath his armpits and hauled him up into the air, flying awkwardly with him dangling from between my legs.

"Brielle, no. I'm too heavy!" Lincoln roared as I skimmed the tree line and left the cemetery. He *was* heavy—it felt like I was carrying a car—but I was also pumped with "mommy juice", the stuff mothers had when they protected their child or loved one. I had it right then, coursing through my veins in a rush. I could have lifted a freaking semi off a baby deer if I'd had to.

"Mind over matter," I spit out.

I was pretty sure I'd given myself a hernia, as something in my stomach felt like it'd ripped when I lifted him, but I'd deal with that later.

"You won't make it to Fallen Academy. Go into the war zone. Michael is on patrol tonight," Lincoln called out over the wind.

I could see the wall and the fiery war just behind it to my right, much closer than Fallen Academy. Flapping my wings in that direction, I veered us toward the war and prayed Michael would be there to rescue me. I'd just remembered that I'd created a Celestial orb, and I was going to crash *very* soon.

Just then, something wrapped around my ankle, jerking me backward. The sudden movement caused Lincoln to slip in my arms and I... I dropped him.

I dropped him right over the war zone.

Oh God.

"Lincoln!" I screamed until my voice was hoarse.

It was only about a twenty-foot drop, but his wings weren't out. *At this height, will he break his legs? Oh, Lincoln!*

"Like I said, you're coming with me," Lucifer called from behind me.

'Castrate him already!' Sera screamed, flaring to life.

Anger snapped inside of me and I felt the darkness blaze within me. Raphael was right. I was feeding the darkness. I was angry, but not at the world, or Raphael, or even God. I was mad at this asshole right in front of me.

"Ahhhh!" I screamed as my face shook with rage and hot black magic flew from my throat, wrapping around Lucifer's head. The second it hit his face, it dissolved, as if it were unable to harm him.

Oh frick.

"Yes!" Lucifer shouted with pride, pulling on the black rope that held my ankle. "You will make a great archdemon," he purred.

Archdemon.

It's true? This whole time...it was true.

Tiffany's stupid blond face popped into my head then and I wanted to cry.

"No, she won't," a familiar voice called out, and then a streak of blue light cut through the black band around my leg, like it was lightning.

"Hello, old friend." Lucifer grinned in Archangel Michael's direction.

Michael wasted no words, just flew at the Devil blindingly fast until they crashed together like two meteors exploding in the sky.

That's when the fatigue hit me. The Celestial ball, flying with Lincoln, it had zapped every last ounce of energy I possessed, and suddenly I was falling.

Landing in Lincoln's arms was the last thing I saw.

CHAPTER 23

WHEN I CAME TO, THERE WERE HUSHED VOICES. My mouth felt dry, and I had practically melted into the bed with exhaustion. Peeling my eyes open, I saw it actually wasn't a bed but a sleeping bag, and I was in a tent.

"I think he's fled back to the underworld." Lincoln's voice was strong, and I nearly cried hearing it. He was okay.

"I'm not taking any chances. The other archangels are coming to escort Brielle back to the academy, which is where she'll need to stay." Michael's voice was fatigued and sharp.

"Yes. Thank you, sir," Lincoln replied.

"Linc," I mumbled loudly, wondering how many

hours had passed. I needed water and a ten-hour nap.

Lincoln burst into the tent then, and I was surprised to see he looked relatively unharmed.

"You're okay," he breathed.

I nodded. If by okay, he meant the Devil was chasing me and I felt like I'd been hit by a truck, then yeah, I was okay.

He knelt down beside me.

"What happened? Lucifer? Your wings?" I asked, sitting up slowly. I reached down to my thigh to do a quick check and make sure Sera was still with me. Then my eyes fell to the small diamond band on my left finger and I smiled.

I'm promised.

Lincoln rolled out his shoulder. "They're broken, but Noah says they'll heal in time. I just can't use them." He was a soldier. Without his wings, he could get hurt.

"Lucifer?" I asked again.

Anger lit up Lincoln's face. "Gone for now. But Brielle…" He was having a hard time composing himself.

I nodded. "I heard. I can't leave Fallen Academy for a while."

His eyes went cobalt. "Forever."

I recoiled. "*What?*"

Lincoln grasped my hands. "Brielle, it's the only place you can be safe."

272

I puffed air through my teeth. "I'm a Fallen Army soldier. How can I help with the war if I'm hiding on campus?"

Lincoln sighed and looked out the tent's open flap. "You can run the healing clinic or advise."

Advise? What the hell did that even mean? I knew he was trying to help, and I did want to focus on my healing studies, but I also wanted to be out there, in the war zones, ferrying the people into Angel City.

"So I just hide for the rest of my life?" My voice felt hollow, and in that moment, the Dark Prince's words came back to me.

Archdemon. I'm an archdemon.

'*Oh hooey, what does that shit-for-brains know?*' Sera voiced, but I couldn't get that dark thought out of my mind. It had latched on tightly, and now I felt it would consume me.

Lincoln ran a hand through his hair. "No, you can't hide for the rest of your life. Look, we'll figure this out, okay? For the next two years, you'll stay on campus and... We'll figure this out."

Two years.

"Can I still sleep over on weekends?" Technically his apartment was just off campus.

He swallowed hard. "The demon alarm doesn't extend to my apartment complex, so..."

My face fell. Next year everyone would be getting apartments, and I'd be stuck in the dorms.

"But I'll see about getting you your own room, or I'll buy you a trailer," he rambled.

He was being agreeable, so I would decide to stay on campus. I knew him too well. But I also didn't want to get kidnapped by the Devil, and taken to Hell to do God knew what, and become some archdemon. I just nodded. I'd do what was best for me and for Lincoln.

'*Good girl,*' Sera agreed.

There was a bright light at the tent opening, and then Raphael was ducking his head in, to peek inside. His chest was adorned in full gold-plated armor and his hair was slicked back into a ponytail. I'd never seen him battle-ready, but he looked menacing.

"Hello, Brielle. Let's get you home."

Nodding once more, I stood with Lincoln's help, and then walked out of the tent to greet the four archangels.

The first thing I saw was Michael's face and hair streaked with black oil and soot. When he saw me approach, he bowed slightly. "Brave Brielle. I'm very proud of what you did."

My eyes widened, and I just barely resisted the urge to look over my shoulder and see if he was talking to someone else. I'd made a half-good, half-evil orb, then wussed out and flew away. What could he possibly be proud of?

Michael seemed to read my thoughts. "Lucifer invokes fear in people, but you didn't cow. You fought, and then, when you knew it would be useless to fight any longer, you retreated."

All of the archangels nodded in agreement.

"Carrying Lincoln that high, and that far. It takes tremendous strength," Raphael added.

Mommy juice.

"I guess so." I was too tired to argue.

I looked around, wondering if I'd see a car waiting to take me home. We were in a parking lot of what was once a grocery store, and now seemed to be a temporary military setup. The only cars were a few military-issued SUVs, but they were far off the lot.

"I'm not sure I can walk that far. I'm so exhausted," I told the crowd of powerful archangels with a bit of shame.

Michael stepped forward, wings fully extended. "We'll be flying back to the academy. All of the roads are on lockdown after Lucifer let a bunch of demons into Angel City. The army is still trying to gather them up. Flying is safer."

I wasn't sure I could fly back to the academy either.

As if he'd heard that thought, Lincoln stepped forward. "She's too weak to fly. Michael, can you carry her?" Lincoln asked the tall, blond, and extremely gorgeous archangel.

"Of course." Michael stepped closer to me.

I swallowed nervously. Being the damsel in distress wasn't my thing, but I *was* about to fall over.

Lincoln rushed forward, pressing a tender but chaste kiss to my lips. "I'll check in on you later," he promised.

Michael nodded to Lincoln. "Hold down the fort until I'm back."

Lincoln raised a hand and saluted him. "Of course, sir."

Then Michael was there, gathering me in his arms, and with one kick of his boot, we were airborne. Next thing I knew, Raphael, Gabriel, and the elusive Uriel were flying with us in a protective formation.

I loved Lincoln, I did, and I knew Michael was married, but damn if the situation wasn't a little swoon-worthy. Being ferried across the sky in a strong archangel's arms? I could definitely cross it off my bucket list.

After a short flight, we were landing in the quad where a few students were still milling around, Shea one of them. Lincoln must have called her. Her eyes were rimmed red, evidence that she must have been worried and crying.

As Michael set me down, I looked at each one of the archangels and thanked them. Michael had been the only one to hear Lucifer's words about me being an archdemon, and our gazes lingered a little longer than the others as something unspoken passed between us. That look told me he wouldn't tell anyone what the Prince of Darkness had said.

As they flew away—all but Raph, who walked back to his office—Shea thrust herself at me in a bone-crunching hug.

"What the hell, Bri! One second Lincoln tells me he's proposing to you tonight, and the next he calls and says the freaking Devil crashed your engagement."

Tears lined my eyes as I looked at my best friend's worried gaze. Holding up my hand to show her the ring, I smiled. "I said yes."

We both let out a pathetic laugh, and then she was pulling me toward the open Bright Hall doors. "Dude, your mom is worried sick," Shea informed me as we walked through the halls.

Lots and lots of staring at me confirmed that the rumor mill was in full effect. Tiffany's stare was the only one that got to me though. *If she calls me Archie, I'll kill her dead right here and now.* I lifted my left hand in her direction to show off the ring, and the look she gave me confirmed that she was definitely capable of murder as well.

"Did you guys know Lincoln was going to propose?" I asked my bestie.

She scoffed. "Of course! He sat your mom, Mikey, and me down and asked us all."

My heart nearly melted at her words. He was the best.

When Shea threw open the door to our shared room, I was assaulted with white balloons and toilet paper streamers. Purple magical writing hung in the air above my bed: 'Congrats!'

But the sullen faces of Luke, Chloe, my mom, and Mikey were a different story.

"Hey…" I wasn't sure what else to say.

My mom rushed forward to pull me into a hug. "What happened? Are you okay? Did he hurt you?"

I really, *really* didn't want to talk about it right then. "I'm fine," I told her, and she backed away two steps, seemingly taking the hint.

I held up my hand awkwardly and smiled. "So… Lincoln proposed. Or kind of. Promised? If that's a thing. We're getting married in like three to five years," I told the group.

That seemed to loosen them up. Chloe burst forward with her vampire-like speed and inspected the ring. "Oh my God, I'm so jelly. Promise rings are adorable."

I chuckled.

Luke was next. "I'm super happy for you, and I know this is all about you, but something happened that I've been dying to tell you guys."

Yes. Please take the spotlight off me. "Spill it." I sat on the edge of my bed because if I didn't, I was going to fall over.

Luke looked at Chloe a little awkwardly and then chewed his lip. "Donnie asked me out to a movie with a few of his friends, and I'm freaking out!" He jumped up and down like a lunatic.

I grinned. "That's awesome. Is it like a friendly group hang, or...?"

Luke looked desperately at Chloe. "I don't know. He said, 'You wanna catch a flick with me and my buddies, Tommy and Bam?'"

Chloe nodded, impressed. "Tommy and Bam are dating, so it's totally a double date."

The shriek that left Luke's throat was akin to a dolphin trying to find its mother.

"I'm going to faint," he breathed.

I laughed, as did everyone else. Even my mother was laughing.

"Thanks for being here, guys. I love you all," I told my friends as the exhaustion hit me full steam.

Lying back on my pillow, I tried to keep my eyes open but failed. The last thing I saw was my mother tucking the blanket around me and telling everyone I needed my rest.

Even at twenty years old, a girl still needs her mom.

CHAPTER 24

THE NEXT MORNING, I AWOKE TO A STRONG hand massaging my back. I inhaled and smelled bacon and coffee. My eyelids snapped open and I drank in the sight of my man. Lincoln was sitting on my dorm room bed, rubbing my back in slow, soothing circles.

"Hey, it's afternoon. I wanted to make sure you were okay," he whispered.

I eyed the milky coffee, the plate of eggs and bacon on my dresser, and nodded. "I'm fine now," I declared, shoving two full strips of bacon in my mouth in one go. If a man brought you coffee and bacon in bed, you marry that man.

Lincoln chuckled. "I'm glad to hear it." He wrapped his hand around my left one and spun the ring on my finger. "Not exactly how I thought that night was going to end."

Yeah, tell me about it.

He looked around the room at the balloons and toilet paper. "At least it looks like you got a little celebration."

I chugged the coffee, feeling my soul finally join my body, something only coffee was capable of doing. "This is my life. Black wings, devil marks and...what happened last night." I wanted him to know what he was in for.

Lincoln frowned. "But it won't always be. This war is going to end, and we're going to live...forever, really."

Forever.

Whoa.

I'd conveniently forgotten about the immortality thing. Live forever unless killed.

I nodded. "But if it doesn't, and I'm always going to be hunted by him..."

Him. I couldn't even say his name anymore.

Lincoln shrugged. "Then we'll deal with it. Together."

I sighed, nuzzling my head into his neck. He always knew the perfect thing to say.

Tonight was Lincoln's surprise captain's promotion.

I glanced at the clock to see it was already three. I'd slept all day.

'No more Celestial balls. Bad idea, not worth it,' Sera exclaimed.

'Agreed.'

"I should shower," I told Lincoln and peeled back my covers. He looked at my bare legs and his eyes hooded.

"I could use a shower too." He scooped me into his arms, lifting me off the bed.

Laughter erupted from my belly as he walked me into the bathroom. Threading my fingers through his hair, I couldn't help but appreciate how perfect Lincoln Grey was in that moment.

I wanted to freeze it and capture it forever.

———•—•———

That night, Noah snuck me into the reception hall, and I sat at the large white cloth-covered table with Lincoln's closest friends. Lincoln had been on the stage under the guise that he was helping Raphael honor some other Fallen Army soldiers, which they did. But when Raphael introduced his surprise promotion, I started to cry. He'd listed off my man's achievements, including the numerous lives he'd saved, and families he'd brought to the safety of Angel City. It was a beautiful ceremony, and when Lincoln saw I was there, he'd beamed with pride.

Now we were at the after-party. The archangels

had gone home, the music was loud, and Shea, Luke, and Chloe had officially crashed the party.

I was dancing with Lincoln when he leaned into my ear. "I'm thirsty. Want a drink?"

I nodded.

As he made his way off the dance floor, Shea twerked her way over to me, much to the dismay of Noah who had been grinding up on her.

"So, I've been thinking," Shea shouted over the music. "If you're stuck on campus for the next few years, I'd bet we could convince Raph to give us our own dorm rooms next year, right next to each other."

I smiled. "Really? You'd stay in the lame dorms with me, even though everyone else will be getting apartments?"

Shea nodded. "What can I say? I'm just that good of a friend."

I laughed. She really was and I told her so.

After a nod, she leaned in closer. "Did you hear that Fallen Academy will only be open for a few more years? After that, all of the children left will be human."

Her declaration shocked the crap out of me. I quickly did the math and realized she was right. I was five when the war started, so five years after entering the academy, the last angel blessed or demon gifted teen would have their Awakening ceremony and then...

"What are they going to do with the school?" I'd

completely stopped dancing by that point, enthralled with the conversation.

Shea looked left and right, as if she was about to reveal some big secret. "I heard Raphael was going to start a demon hunter academy. Training humans."

Whoa.

Humans? I mean, no offense to humans but they were...weak little humans. It would be a waste to just have the school sit there, though, and I was sure we'd still need soldiers for the army.

I nodded. "Yeah, that makes sense."

Shea was about to respond when the shrill of the demon alarm went off.

The music skidded to a halt and my entire body froze.

My best friend's eyes widened. "Is that...?" she asked with a shaky voice.

"Brielle!" Lincoln shouted from across the room.

He was looking not at me but behind me, horror marring his face. I knew then, without a shadow of a doubt, that the Dark Prince was standing behind me, probably with his horde of demons. He wouldn't stop coming for me, I knew that now.

I spun on my heels and faced him. Standing in an immaculate suit—not a dark hair out of place— was Lucifer in all his evil glory. His inky black wings were stretched out behind him, and just as I thought, he had an assortment of Hellhounds, Yew demons, an Abrus, Brimstone, and three or four nauseating

Larkspur demons splayed out beside him. Behind him spun a swirling portal right to Hell—I could smell the sulfur from where I stood.

"Brielle, my darling." Lucifer stepped forward and I moved away from Shea, snapping my wings out to cover her and everyone I loved behind me. Lincoln, Shea, Noah, Chloe, Luke—nearly every person I loved in this world was in the room.

Sera flared to life at my hip, nearly burning my leg.

'You have no idea what I'm capable of,' she told me menacingly.

Holy shit.

'Well, now would be a good time to show me. All of these people could be hurt because of me.'

Sera pulsed as I took her in my hand. *'The greatest power on Earth is love,'* she said, and then my arm raised out before me as the demon horde advanced, and a firewall of light shot from Sera's blade, spreading out like an ocean wave.

I had to dig my heels into the wood floors to keep from sliding backward with the powerful thrust that came from her blade. The Celestial light rose like a tidal wave, completely saturating the Dark Prince and his demons. Hissing and screams rang out as the light washed over them. When it passed, Lucifer was standing in a protective black bubble while the rest of his demons were charred to a crisp.

Holy. Freaking. Shit.

Sera had been holding out on me, but it hadn't been enough. Lucifer was still standing.

Lincoln stepped in front of me suddenly, sword raised. "Back to Hell with you!" he roared, then started to run at the Prince of Darkness. Noah, Blake, and Darren were right behind him.

Idiots!

"Lincoln, no!" The words barely left my mouth when the room exploded.

Lucifer clapped his hands together and then thrust them forward, shooting a million tiny shards of black magic into every single person standing, including me.

It felt like a dozen tiny arrows had sliced through my body.

I fell backward, trying to dodge the black glass-like shards, and that's when Lucifer really brought out the big guns. He lifted his sword into the air, a red fire erupting along the blade, then slammed it down into the hardwood floors, causing an earthquake to split the room into four different pieces. Shea had to jump to avoid falling into the abyss. I saw Lincoln and Noah dive to try to get on the cracked piece that the Dark Prince stood on but they couldn't, their wings banded to their backs with dark magic.

Oh God.

'*Don't panic,*' Sera attempted to calm me.

By the time the room had stopped shaking, Lucifer and I were on the same piece of flooring, only ten feet from each other, with the portal spinning behind him. He snapped his fingers and I started to be pulled in his direction against my will.

'*Okay, let's panic,*' Sera agreed.

"No!" Lincoln roared. His wings snapped out, pushing against the black bands that bound his arms, the sound of absolute agony ripping from his voice.

They're broken! He's trying to pull out broken wings!

I tried to pull my arms up, to aim Sera at the Devil but I couldn't move, completely immobilized. It was at that moment that I realized Lucifer had been toying with me before, taunting me, and waiting for me to be trained so he could grab me when he wanted to. He could have easily taken me that first night in the gauntlet, but he let me stay. Let me fall in love with all of these people, train to be a badass killer, and for what?

I pumped my wings, trying to fight against the strong pull of his lure. Shea threw purple spell after purple spell, but they all crashed into his dark shield, breaking up and causing no harm.

"A young girl with black wings will go into the underworld and kill Lucifer, ending the war," the Dark Prince sneered, and my stomach dropped.

The prophecy.

Did he believe it?

"I can't very well have that, can I?" he asked.

He was going to kill me.

"Brielle!" Lincoln called out one final time, and I spun my head around to see him.

He jumped.

Bless his heart, he jumped the twenty feet, with broken wings and black bands around his upper arms. My heart lurched in my throat. If I had to watch him plummet to his death, I wouldn't survive.

He sailed across the cavern, but he wasn't going to make it. It was short.

Oh God.

With a cry, he wiggled his arm out of the restricting band and at the last second caught the lip of the cavernous surface, barely holding himself up by the fingertips.

I'd reached him now, the Devil, the shit-for-brains asshole who'd ruined my life.

"Lincoln!" I shouted behind me, tears falling down my face. I could no longer see him, didn't know if he was still hanging on.

Lucifer spun me around, holding me tightly to his body, and placed the tip of his sword at my neck. My arms, my legs, everything was cement. I couldn't move, could barely even breathe.

"Say goodbye, Brielle," he taunted as we walked backward, my feet dragging along the top of the wood floors, as I fought my invisible restraints. Sera was pulsing with power but nothing was hurting him.

He was invincible.

This is it. He's going to kill me. I didn't want to go out like that, be remembered like that.

I looked right into Lincoln's eyes as he struggled to climb up over the edge.

"I love you," I told him, then met Shea's, Luke's, and Chloe's gazes as well. "I love you all."

In that moment, Lincoln burst up from the cavern with a roar and started running at us full throttle. Only one arm was freed and so he wasn't able to do anything, not even hold a blade.

"I don't think so, lover boy," Lucifer trilled, then pulled the blade hard against my neck.

Pain sliced along my skin as warm blood trickled down my shirt.

Lincoln's grief-stricken face was the last thing I saw before the portal closed, and everything went black.

———•—•———

Suddenly, a cool hand clamped around my neck, and lights flared to life inside the dark hell cave.

My legs felt weak, and my head swam with the blood loss... I was totally dying.

But that hand around my neck was colder and colder by the minute, and when I smelled the cinnamon and oil, that distinct smell of demon healer magic I gasped a little. The Dark Prince swam into view, plucking Sera from me, and depositing her in a black charcoal type of box with symbols on it.

'Brielle!' She shouted.

I couldn't answer her, I was trying to figure out how I wasn't dead.

"Oh, calm down. I didn't cut you deep enough to kill you." Lucifer admonished.

I was lowered to the ground by cool firm hands and came face to face with a Nubby Horned Healer demon. They were stark white, in every aspect, skin, hair, and eyes and very very rare. It seemed Lucifer didn't want to create too many of them.

As that cinnamon smell swirled around me, and the magic worked its way into my neck, I found myself wondering why. Why would he do this? Fake my death?

"Why?" I croaked.

Lucifer grinned; he was devastatingly handsome which sickened me.

Reaching out, he booped my nose with a sharp fingernail. "Better to give them closure little archdemon. You're never going to see them again."

Oh God.

'Brielle! What's happening?' Sera begged.

The box he'd put her in had somehow dulled her powers. She couldn't see or sense things.

'We're stuck in Hell. Forever. And all my friends think I'm dead.'

READ ON FOR A SNEAK PEEK AT THE NEXT BOOK IN THE FALLEN ACADEMY SERIES

CHAPTER 1

BRIELLE

I MOANED, ROLLING OVER IN BED AND TRYING TO let my eyes adjust. Every morning for the past month it was the same thing: I woke up in Hell, in my little stone room, all drugged up and discombobulated, seeing double and feeling ill.

"Morning. Time for your meds," Raksha told me.

I glared at the Dark Mage. We had a love-hate relationship. She wasn't abusive or overly rude; she only did what the Dark Prince told her, and yet she was still my captor.

"No more drugs, please," I whimpered.

The meds made me feel sluggish, depressed, and sick.

She mixed my oatmeal, her dark hair falling around her face, making her look pretty. She was a woman of Indian descent, about mid-thirties, and terribly powerful. The first day I was here, I'd tried to blast her with my magic and she'd thrown me across the room, reopening my neck wound.

She tsked between her teeth. "You know the rules, child. You take the meds, and then you can see the Dark Prince."

"I don't want to see the fucking prince!" I snapped.

Her eyes snapped up to me, and a red haze came over them. When she stood and stalked over to me with the oatmeal in her hand, she wore a look of determination.

"I'm going to let you in on a little secret. You want to survive down here? Then you do what he says. You understand?" Something in her voice, in her face, changed to the point that she almost seemed like a decent human being. But that all ended when she shoved the first spoon of 'oatmeal' into my mouth, and clamped my lips shut.

"Swallow," she growled.

I looked down at my left hand, the ring that sat there. She'd been the one to let me keep it. The Dark Prince thought it might be spelled, but she'd looked it over, declared it useless, and suggested it might motivate me if I could have it. They'd taken the pendant Mr. Claymore made me, but at least they'd let me hold on to the ring.

I swallowed the medicated breakfast, letting it slide down my throat.

Lincoln.

God, that name. Just the thought of him brought tears to my eyes, as a physical pain opened in my chest. Did he think I was dead? What was Shea doing? My mom? Mikey?

Tears flowed down my cheeks, and Raksha smacked my hand.

"None of that weakness in here. Swallow it down. Survive," she barked.

There were glimpses, like this one, where I actually thought she was trying to help me.

"Why the meds still? I haven't tried to attack the Dark Prince in a few days," I attempted to reason with her as she shoved another spoonful in my mouth.

Raksha gave me a glare. "A few days? Let's try a few weeks, and then maybe I'll be permitted to cut the meds."

A few more weeks down here? Oh God, I couldn't imagine that. I'd lose my mind.

The meds made it so I couldn't do magic, couldn't fly, couldn't talk to Sera. That last one killed me the most out of all of them. Knowing she was down here with me, but our connection was suppressed.

"Okay, I won't fight him anymore. I see now that it's useless." I would have to try another way to get out of here. Play it like I was on their side.

She nodded, spooning the gritty and bitter oatmeal into my mouth. "Good girl. Do as you're told."

ACKNOWLEDGMENTS

I apologize for the ending, I promise I didn't mean to torture you; it just happened. Thank you to Amanda Rose for the amazing cover. Big thanks to my beta readers, Steven Smithen, Lela Eder, and Megan Mayes (especially for helping me with the ending lol). Thank you to Hot Tree Editing for the amazing edits and to my wonderful proofreader Stephany Wallace for polishing this baby. A HUGE thank-you, as always to my loving and supportive family. The time I spend with my characters is time away from you all and I'm so grateful you understand this passion I have for writing. Lastly, to my ARC team, Leia Stone Wolf Pack, and all my readers, thank you for being so loyal and enthusiastic about my books. I heart you all bad. <3

ABOUT THE AUTHOR

Leia Stone is the *USA Today* bestselling author of multiple bestselling series, including Matefinder, Wolf Girl, The Gilded City, Fallen Academy, and Kings of Avalier. She's sold over three million books, and her Fallen Academy series has been optioned for film. Her novels have been translated into multiple languages and she even dabbles in script writing.

Leia writes urban fantasy and paranormal romance with sassy kick-butt heroines and irresistible love interests. She lives in Spokane, Washington, with her husband and two children.

Instagram: @leiastoneauthor
TikTok: @leiastone
Facebook: leia.stone
Website: www.LeiaStone.com